BLACK HEART

MOIRA KANE

For every bird that broke free of her cage.

Content Warning

Dear reader,

Thanks for reading Black Heart. Before you begin, please be aware of the following potential triggers:

-*Physical and emotional abuse*

-*Scars/scarring*

-*Non-consensual sexual acts (mentioned but not depicted)*

-*Violence and gore*

DISTANT SHORES
SPEARTIP BREACH
ESKALI CITADEL
ESKALI FJORD
RYDAR
STARBORN GLADES
WAR CAMPS
STARBORN
SILVER ORE PORT
BURNE'S SECRET
SILVER SEA
SILVER COAST
CAPE OF CASTREL
GAZAR
GREY JUNGLE
GAZARI PORT

Sapphire Mines
Yore
Port of Yore
Forgotten King
Ghost Lands
The Winter Wilds
The Clans
War Camps
The Black Estate
Brula
Brulian Port
The Blackwood
Brilend
The Briarwood
The Frozen Shore
Calos Valley
Port of Calos
SVALTA

CHAPTER 1

MARA

"**N**OT A PARTICULARLY CHARMING man," Queen Sophia waved her hand as if to swat a bug. "Your betrothed, I mean."

Mara hadn't known what to expect when the Queen of Calos requested a private audience with her the morning before the first of many celebratory wedding feasts. She was often responsible for entertaining her father's guests, serving tea and cakes while discussing the petty topics she had tightly memorized. None had been guests so important as the rulers of Calos, their furthest neighbor to the south, and none had wanted privacy.

If anything, an audience was expected. Ladies in waiting from the wealthy courtier families that had more marriageable daughters than they had dowries were placed like props around the room, their colorful skirts billowing over expensive but uncomfortable stools. Mara always suspected they were made that way on purpose. Having to perch awkwardly on a round cushion that was two sizes too small required excellent posture and balance, preventing a lady from slouching and lounging.

Without the proper attendants, how was a lady to prove she was the most well-informed gossip? That her connections stretched far and wide through the court? That she was affluent enough to be wearing the latest fashion? A queen, Mara supposed, need not prove herself to anyone. She was already the wealthiest and most elegantly dressed woman when she walked into any room.

Or she should have been. It wasn't that Queen Sophia was ill dressed, only that her attire was not fitting of early autumn. Perhaps fashion trends were different in Calos? The gown that adorned the queen's tall, lithe form was a brilliant shade of ruby—the right color for autumn, at the very least. The style, however, was bordering on immodest.

Mara was reminded of a drawing of women from a century ago during her history lessons. They wore gowns that hung low on their shoulders too, the dips and curves of their breasts on display. Women were afforded more freedom of dress in those times. More freedom of every facet. Again, she remembered that Sophia was a queen and queens were welcome to do as they pleased, so long as their husbands allowed it.

Lucilla, her stepmother, certainly did. Quietly, secretly, Mara sometimes wondered if perhaps Lucilla was doing more than her husband approved of. A busy, distracted king didn't make for a good leader in his marriage.

"Sophia," King Burne chided his wife.

"I'm a queen. I can say what I wish."

"Don't let her fool you. She spoke out of term just as often before she was a queen," Burne whispered conspiratorially, shocking Mara with his informal speech. Queen Sophia turned her flailing hand on him like he was the bug. He caught it, landing kisses on each of her knuckles, his eyes glittering with affection. She smiled back at him in a manner much too sultry for a queen.

"I'm told he's an excellent diplomat." Mara said with a polite smile. "How lovely to see such felicity in an arranged match. You both seem terribly happy."

"Oh, our marriage wasn't arranged," Burne corrected, his words rich with fondness. "I swept her off her feet."

"Quite literally," Sophia added, meeting his gaze as if they shared a delicious secret between the two of them.

Mara's smile was more genuine then, hopefully disguising the yearning that clawed up from her chest in an attempt to perch on her features like an unsightly bird.

"That sounds very romantic." And surprising. Royalty did not often, if ever, marry for love. If Mara were lucky, her future husband would be someone she could grow to love in time.

Pity softened the queen's brow, and Mara winced. She must have been too obvious. With a shallow breath, Mara steadied herself, schooling her face until she wore the mask of a poised princess.

"Do you want to marry him?"

Mara's mask held steady. "I am pleased with the match my father arranged for me, your highness."

"Oh, please! You're more than a bargaining chip, princess. They might try to sell you like a prized mare, but that doesn't mean you have to trot obediently behind them."

"You're being rather uncouth, love."

"I'm being honest." Sophia tutted. "Do you want to know the real reason your father invited us? It is not to fill the table at your wedding feast with royal company."

"Sophia!" The king shook his head.

"I'm a queen—"

Burne interrupted, his exasperation warring with amusement. "You can't use that as an excuse each time you insult and berate people."

"I'm doing neither. She deserves to know she has options. Don't forget, I bore the same burden as her once." Sophia's countenance shifted, becoming deadly serious. "Ask me. Don't you want to know why we're here?"

"Why are you here?" Mara asked automatically.

"Your father wants to know how I tamed the dragon of Calos Valley." Mara was curious herself, but hadn't thought it proper to ask. "My grandfather was famous for slaying a dragon, but he was a man, and men are violent and stupid."

Burne cleared his throat but said nothing.

"When the sky darkens, and the air rumbles with monstrous roars, the people of Calos are unafraid. My dragon is our protector."

"And you think you can teach my father to tame the dragon that has claimed the Blackwood for decades?" Mara felt like a wide-eyed child. Sophia was a brave woman, fierce as the dragon she ruled over. If only Mara could embody a fraction of that strength.

"It's not wrong to claim what is rightfully yours." Burne grumbled. "If you're planning what I think you're planning, I would advise against it. This is not a wise idea, Sophia. A dragon is not *tamed* by just anyone." In a voice that Mara suspected she wasn't meant to hear, he added, "Especially this one, grumpy lout."

"Maybe not, but a dragon is honorable enough to help a woman in need."

"*Some* dragons. This one...well, it's been many years since I've last heard—" The king cleared his throat. "Heard of the Blackwood dragon." He turned his attention to Mara. "Has anyone seen him in recent years?"

She considered. "There are rumors from those who venture through the outskirts of the Blackwood on trade routes, but it is not my place to say which is true. When I was a child, the sightings were frequent." The creature blasted through the sky almost daily. As terrifying as the beast's presence had been, Mara always felt a strange kinship with him. He was clearly angry—so very angry—and was hungry for destruction. Perhaps for retaliation against whoever or whatever angered him so.

Though her rage was impotent, tucked away and untouched for years, Mara understood. If she could take to the sky with great wings, she would. If her hands were decorated with sharp talons and her mouth with even sharper teeth, she would destroy buildings and slaughter livestock, too. Such thoughts were improper for a princess, however, and it was easier if she suppressed them lest she let that hateful emotion get the better of her.

"Tell me, princess, will Baron Black be attending your wedding?"

The question was so off topic that she was speechless for a heartbeat. Blinking back her befuddlement, she answered, "I...er, no. No, your highness." Feeling foolish for her sputtered response, Mara added, "Baron Black has scarcely been heard from in years. The family Black is stubbornly rooted in their estate deep in the Blackwood. Some fear they will be devoured by the dragon if they try to leave."

"Yes, that sounds right. Gannon always was a stubborn prick."

"I beg your pardon?"

"Forgive me, princess. It seems my sweet wife's rotten vocabulary is rubbing off on me." Burne smiled, his white teeth gleaming in contrast to his tan skin. He was a very handsome man. Mara could see why the queen was taken with him. "If the need were to arise, the Gannon I knew would shelter a maiden on a journey westward. But many, many years have passed since I spoke with him. I cannot judge his state of mind now."

Sophia smiled wickedly. "She will have to decide for herself if it's worth the risk."

Were they truly discussing this? Mara leaving—*escaping,* as it were—and joining them in Calos. Why? For what purpose would they want her? She'd scarcely spoken to the queen for two minutes before Sophia was plotting to send her to Baron Black.

Mara had never met any members of house Black, but she'd heard enough gossip to know that none of the four brothers were the most desirable company for a princess on the run from her responsibility. The Baron was rumored to be curt, bordering on cruel. Of the four, he was the sole member of their family that fulfilled his stately duties after the late Baron, their father, journeyed onward to the heavens.

"Is this a trick?" Mara blurted, hardly caring that she was being rude.

"No tricks." Sophia's expression was solemn. "I only wish to offer you the freedom that Lady Fate granted me. A marriage arranged for monetary value, to move territory markers, or add trade routes to faraway places, is wrong. Women are not treasure to be exchanged for political favor."

"Are we going to rescue every young girl who wants out of an arranged marriage?" Burne interrupted.

"Maybe so." She lifted her chin regally. "It's about time fathers stopped selling their daughters to foreign men. If your kind has the right to choose a mate," Sophia pointed to Mara, "Then so does her kind."

"And what will happen when royal bloodlines end with princesses marrying peasants?" Burne arched a brow, his tone rich with a humor Mara didn't understand.

"Necessary change, I imagine." The queen rose on the tips of her toes, barely able to reach her husband's lips even then. Mara blushed and turned away from the show of affection. "Stop being so unromantic. Let the girl have a choice."

"*You* haven't even asked the girl if she wants a choice."

"Fair point." Intent blue eyes bounced to her, drilling through that perfect princess mask and peeking into her soul. "Do you wish to marry?"

Yes. She thought instantly. *I wish to marry someone with a beautiful heart. Someone that will look to me the way your king does to you. I wish to marry a man that won't wander from our marriage bed when making love to a princess has lost its novelty.*

"I...Forgive me..."

"You are a person before you are a princess." The queen clicked her tongue. "Do you wish to marry the man your father has chosen for you?"

The word tumbled from her lips before Mara could stop it. "No."

Sophia took her hands. "Do you wish to be free of the burden your title places on you?"

"Yes." *Unworthy.* Mara was so unworthy of that title. This was not the way a princess behaved. To even allow such thoughts into her mind was dissent. Punishable. Violent trembles took her body as it recalled each and every punishment she'd received for fulfilling her duties poorly, for thinking improper thoughts and speaking improper words.

"I mean, no!" Mara yanked her hands free and stepped back two paces. "I am so very honored to be wed to Lord Wyman. So very honored..." The last sentence came out as a whisper fit for a mouse.

"What have they done to you?" Burne was the one that spoke up, his brow hard as stone, his eyes seeming to lighten and shimmer.

"You have a choice, whether they let you believe it." Queen Sophia took her husband's hand. "If you wish to be free of this marriage contract, we will see to it that you are released, one way or another. And if you wish to leave this place, you have a home in Calos. I should welcome a lady with a head for court politics. Gods, I am so terrible with those awful courtiers. I have half a mind to feed them to my dragon."

"She'll need a distraction." The king mused, focusing his attention back on Mara. Both of them watched her too intently, making her wish she could become the mouse she sounded like and scurry away. There was a predatory weight to Burne's gaze. It reminded her of the tiger father had once kept to entertain and intimidate his guests. The creature would watch the crowd hungrily, anticipating a chance to strike.

"I have an excellent one in mind." Sophia's smirk was a match to the tiger's.

Chapter 2

Mara

WOMEN SCREAMED, SOME FAINTING into the arms of nearby noblemen. Goblets of wine were knocked over as men rushed to swords that were used more for décor than dealing death. The screech and thump of a heavy wooden table toppling forward echoed somewhere in the hall. To his credit, Mara's betrothed was one of those bravely armed, his body turned as if to protect her.

Doubt crept in to gnaw at the resolve Mara thought she'd molded earlier that evening. Perhaps Lord Wyman was a good man, worth giving a chance. He was an excellent diplomat, well respected and reasonably wealthy. What if Mara could come to love him and him to love her?

Overhead, a dragon bellowed for a second time, reminding her that whatever her choice, it had to be made quickly. Decades passed with relative peace since the Beast of Blackwood showed his face over the city, and the people were unprepared for the frightening presence that made the wooden beams overhead groan as if they too would buckle in fear.

Distraction. Queen Sophia gracefully exited her chair and headed for the great doors to the hall, unthreatened by the beast tormenting the air above the castle. *They are offering me a distraction.*

Mara swept the room with her gaze, expecting to see Burne playing along with sword drawn. The king was nowhere to be seen.

She couldn't trouble herself with his whereabouts now. Two choices were scrambling for her attention on the tabletop, their insistent feet stomping right over her blood pudding.

Pick me! I am the wisest of us both, each one seemed to say.

When her father took a second bride, naming her stepmother queen, Mara spent those first weeks wondering what life a bird led. How did it feel to spread wings and soar as high and as far as you desired? To be unshackled by obligation and title?

"Your Highness!" Sophia's bold voice carried over the din, quieting the clatter with surprising ease as she spoke to the King of Dunhill. "You didn't invite me and expect I would come alone, did you?" The queen smiled delightedly at Lord Wyman. "My lord, I present a wedding gift greater than any that can be bought. The thrill of entertainment only a dragon can provide."

The earth shook beneath Mara's feet, and she imagined a mountain had uprooted itself and taken a heavy step. Sophia motioned for the guards to throw open the doors. Reluctantly, they obeyed, revealing a horrible and magnificent sight. Through the throngs of terrified courtiers, Mara caught only a brief glimpse of the massive golden wings that were spanning the courtyard. If she drew closer, she would no doubt see a maw lined with teeth the size of daggers.

Memories of the Blackwood Beast soaring overhead were vivid in her mind, but she couldn't recall him ever appearing so large. This dragon was immense in his stature, large enough to eat a horse and still hunger for more.

And Queen Sophia was approaching him as if he were her favorite hunting dog, hand outstretched and shoulders relaxed. Mara longed to have even a pebble of that bravery. That boldness.

Clarity pounded into her, and she reached across the table with her mind, drawing one of her choices from its teasing dance and taking it into her chest. Her life was defined by the family she was born into, by the stone that surrounded her, by the cruel woman that tormented her until she became little more than a speaking doll.

Until today.

Today, Mara would define her own life in the most daring, treacherous way.

The layout of the castle hadn't changed since her stepmother was crowned. Though she was no longer allowed to wander, Mara could recall each and every twist and turn of the hallway, every step it took to reach the kitchen. The staff that were moments ago bustling and sweating over giant pots of stew had taken up position like statues, each bearing different ranges of emotion from fear to fascination.

Her arrival in the kitchen doorway broke the spell, sending each person into a different reaction. Some charged down the hall from where she came, hoping to catch a glimpse of the Dragon of Calos Valley. Others saw her fisted skirt, pale complexion, and heaving chest and took off in the same direction Mara was headed, assuming she was running for her life. The rest huddled behind tables and sacks of flour, hoping to remain untouched if the dragon stormed the castle and ate every person in sight.

Reaching the stable took much longer than she anticipated, her heavy skirts weighing her down as much as her anxiety. By now, someone had to have noticed she was missing. Any second, guards would come rushing through the castle, hunting down the missing princess.

The staff exodus must have reached the stable, spurring the stable boys to run to or from the commotion in the main courtyard. Not a single horse was prepared for a ride, but she hadn't the time or strength to heave a saddle onto an animal's back and figure out how to properly fasten it. If her choice was to be brave and chase freedom, Mara could not hold herself back.

Panic breathed hotly at her nape as she raced down the first row of stalls, searching for a horse that was short enough for her to mount unassisted. *In a gown.* Gods, what was she thinking?

Birds. She was thinking of beautiful wild birds.

The horse she selected snickered restlessly when the metal latch to the door slid from its sheath. Obviously, men were not the only creatures afeared of dragons. Mara cooed and clicked softly at the animal, circling carefully lest she be trampled to death. The Gods were watching over her, as the mare she picked was mild and patient, even as fear puffed from her nostrils in quick breaths.

As gracefully as was manageable in the gown that hung heavily from shoulder to ankle, Mara climbed the side of the horse stall and flung her leg toward the mare's middle. Her booted foot scarcely made it over the animal's back, leaving her straddled between horse and stall, scrambling to hoist herself high enough to mount.

The sudden trumpeting of the dragon overhead startled them both, sending the mare jolting forward without warning. Mara released her hold on the stall, grabbing for the mare's mane and holding on for dear life. A fierce shake of the animal's head let Mara know that she was not pleased with the tight hold, or the way Mara used it to right herself. As soon as Mara was level, the mare kicked up her feet, bolting from the stall and down the long stable.

Cool night air rushed to greet them. Steering the mare away from the castle and toward the side gate, which Mara knew was open for staff coming and going with supplies, was difficult without reins. It was mostly the mare's memory of familiar paths and her growing panic that drove them down the dirt road that led out of the castle walls and through the city. When she needed the mare to change directions, Mara took to tapping her thick neck with a closed fist. It worked—mostly.

Wind battered her face, her surroundings impossible to take in as they flew by. Mara couldn't be sure if she was being pursued. Any noise was drowned out by the roar of blood pumping in her ears. That roar grew louder and more vicious when they exited the last narrow gate that kept the city enclosed, heading straight for the entrance to the Blackwood.

The forest was aptly named. Not a drop of moonlight spilled over the thick canopy to brighten the floor below. Mara's horse came to a skidding stop just before passing the first line of trees, shaking her head and whinnying anxiously. She couldn't blame the horse. The worst of the inhabitants of the Blackwood was a dragon, but he was not the only predator.

Cougars, wolves, and all manner of scavengers lurked in those shadows. There were also robbers and poachers willing to risk the ire of a dragon to earn a few coins. Even beneath the summer sun, she would be foolish to venture in there alone—or at all. What would possibly drive her to journey in there at night, with nothing but the dress she wore and a saddle-less horse?

"Do you know the way to the Black Estate?" Burne asked her that morning.

"Yes." It was only theoretical knowledge, though, learned from many hours spent studying geography with her tutor.

"Take the road to the Black Estate. Make no detours and be quick. Gannon will know of your arrival before you reach his gates."

As she hovered before the Blackwood, Mara realized that she was putting far too much faith in King Burne and Queen Sophia. They were allies, but that didn't mean they wouldn't have underhanded political motives. All nobles did, in Mara's experience. Perhaps this was a plan to end her life or to kidnap her. Perhaps they wanted to end her father's line as a precursor to claiming Dunhill and expanding their rule.

A bird would not be afraid to take a leap of faith, a tiny, fierce voice whispered to her. *She would trust that her wings would catch her if she fell too far.*

"I wish to fly." She said to the road that stretched into the fathomless cloud of ink before her. The mare was in disagreement, bucking wildly on the first tap of Mara's heel and nearly sending her flying. She clung tight to the animal's mane, digging her knees into her mare's ribs. The heel of her boot came down on the horse's flank again, and she shouted, "He-ya!"

With one last stubborn flick of her head, the horse leaped forward, vanishing into the Blackwood.

CHAPTER 3

DESPITE LONG, CURLED CLAWS and sleek, broad wings, he was soundless as he circled the edge of the dirt road. A snake slithering into the path of the oncoming traveler. A very large, very unfriendly snake.

Lately, the divide between the two halves of himself seemed to be widening. What was once a small crack was rapidly becoming a yawning canyon. An abyss with nothing but violence and despair filling it. The dragon had a mind of its own, a hunger for some unattainable fantasy. One that was utterly destroyed a decade earlier when the love of his life—his mate, the purpose for his existence—betrayed him.

The dragon would never accept that it was because of him they were slowly descending into madness. Because of him, they would wither away from loneliness. And Gannon would never accept the dragon's dispute of that claim. He would never accept the beast's vehement disapproval of the one that was *theirs*. Man and dragon were at an impasse, one that would inevitably destroy them both.

Unfortunately for the stranger braving the perilous Blackwood, it would likely end them as well.

Dragons of the Black line were especially skilled hunters under the cover of night. His pupils dilated, opening to receive the faintest glimmers of light dropping down from the heavens and catching the first silhouette of a horse blindly following the road that led to the

Black Estate. Rarely did a traveler come this way by accident. Even more rare was a traveler venturing to his family home on purpose.

The most prominent scent that came to him was equine, sweaty and pouring out familiar notes of pungent clover blossoms and over-ripe fruit—fear. Both horse and rider were equally brave and stupid. Despite their trepidation, they marched onward through the dark.

Yes, the rider was frightened too, his heartbeat thundering loud as the horse's hooves. Fear was a more delicate fragrance on him, mingling with underlying hints of rose petal and honey and something darker—something delicious.

Suddenly he went rigidly still, freezing mid-step, lungs expanding as he breathed in as deeply as he could. His heart rose from the steady *thump-thump* of a predator lying in wait to a beast crazed by thrill. Finally, *finally*, it was happening. This moment he'd waited for from the time he learned to shift from man to dragon.

No. That wasn't possible. For Gannon, that moment had already happened. Fate dealt him a worthless hand. It was done.

Wrong, the dragon hissed his disagreement. That was the problem. The most important choice that would ever be made, and the beast had rejected Madeline when the time came to make their bond. Ungrateful bastard.

Now was not the time to dredge up the past. The rider was almost upon them, and his dragon was ready to pounce. Only, he wouldn't be devouring a trespasser. He would be snatching her from her steed and taking her back to the Black Estate, where she belonged.

She. The rider was a woman. What kind of woman was taking the road through the Blackwood at night, unaccompanied? WoOnlyuld she be a thief? An assassin? What purpose could she possibly have to take such a brash risk?

Gannon was compelled to find out. The whirling mass of loneliness and hatred burned darkly under his sternum, and the sole cure for that pain was riding straight for him. Whoever she was, she would wash him clean. She would set him free from the cage he'd trapped himself in.

No, she wouldn't, because she wasn't his. Gannon had found and lost what he was looking for. This woman would not be her.

⁕

*M*ARA

One minute Mara's horse was trotting carefully along the dirt road, her eyes having adjusted slightly to the devouring darkness of the Blackwood. The next Mara was sliding backward too fast to catch herself as the mare reared up with a desperate cry of fear. Hooves clomped down inches from Mara's head and on instinct, she rolled left toward the trees, hoping the underbrush that was clawing at the narrow dirt road would deter the horse and save her from being trampled.

Thorns and textured leaves grabbed at the fabric of her dress, making her feel as if the plants were trying to drag her further into the unknown of the pathless forest. Their sharp branches were teeth that would chew her up, the darkness a frightening maw that would swallow her whole. Claustrophobic panic tightened her lungs, and she lay in a tangled mess, breathless, until the pounding of hooves snapped her out of it.

"Wait!" She bolted upright, shouting to the spooked animal in utter futility.

In the blink of an eye, her only hope of making it out of the forest by dawn vanished as smoke on the wind. Mara stood, losing half the fabric of her dress to various vines as she did. Hurriedly, she wrenched free from the grasping flora and shuffled onto the road. Or she thought it was the road. Abandoned and unmoving, the surrounding shadows seemed to be closing in on her. The visual disturbance was disorienting, and she struggled to see more than a few feet in front of her.

This was the road, wasn't it? There were no plants rooting in the earth, save for a brave scattering of weeds that were reaching hungrily for the places where sun must penetrate the canopy in the daytime.

The trouble was that Mara didn't know if she should continue to take it. Horses were easily spooked, and the animal could have run off because a bat swooped too close to her head. But the autumn air was growing more frigid as the night stretched on and there weren't bats out this time of year. An owl, perhaps? The shadow of a tree branch?

Dread tickled up from the base of her spine, settling on her nape and making the fine hairs there tingle. Mara had the unmistakable feeling she was being watched. Watched the way her father's miserable tiger watched her, a hungry creature ready to wait an eternity if it meant that one chance to strike.

She wasn't alone in the Blackwood, and whatever was with her was drawing nearer.

Mara sensed more than heard the parting of shrubs and ferns to her right. There was constant movement from the shadows of trees as their branches swayed in the whisper of autumn's cool breath. That inky dance made it nearly impossible to tell who or what was there. But it *was* there.

A hiss sounded from directly in front of her, a sharp exhale that became barely visible steam. Hot breath. Very hot, because the cloud was thick as smoke and triple the size of the small puffs leaving Mara's own mouth.

Another hiss of steam and the shadows suddenly coalesced, shifting until they took the unmistakable form of a beast. A long, serpentine body stretched from the cover of the trees; delicate wings tucked neatly along it. The thick legs that dropped down between those wings were muscled and armed at the base with claws that could easily tear through leather. Mara tracked along those onyx scales, taking in every lethal inch of dragon until she reached his head.

Compared to the dragon she'd caught a glimpse of earlier tonight, this one was small. Small was a relative term when it came to dragons, of course, because his presence still loomed over her the way only a predator could. Cat-like eyes glowed a brilliant green, two emeralds seated in the same infinite black that made up the night sky. Beautiful, mesmerizing gems that saw everything from the tears in her gown to the trembling thump of the pulse point on her jugular.

His head was rather cat-like too; a pointed nose, diamond-shaped features, what were likely horns taking place where triangular ears would be on a feline. Mara was struck with a strangely calming thought. If this was how she died, she would be glad. Not to be dead, but to be witness to such otherworldly beauty up close. It was the first and only time in her life that she was truly awestruck.

How treacherous and terrible beauty could be.

"I am honored to see you." She told the Beast of the Blackwood. "The stories do justice only to your violent deeds, not your divine beauty."

He blinked in response, nostrils flaring as another of those hissing breaths left him. It sounded rather like the bellows of a forge as they were pumped up and down.

Mara lifted her hand, hoping to still him for one more heartbeat, two if she were exceptionally lucky. She took in a great breath of her own, memorizing every flavor of autumn in the air. The wet sweetness of decaying leaves, the clean sting of cool air—the hot charcoal scent of dragon. Charcoal and wild ginger and warmth, if it had a scent.

"Let it be known that I died with my wings spread." She prayed to the Gods above her, the Gods she would soon spend her eternity serving in the heavens. "Let me be remembered as a bird uncaged."

The dragon moved lightning fast, as if he'd been giving her a chance to say her final words before making a meal of her. Rather thoughtful for a murderous beast.

A blistering hand wrapped around her waist, the tips of claws pressing threateningly into her flesh. Another hand reached out to grip her. Unable to watch her own end coming at her, Mara squeezed her eyes shut.

She didn't see the thick muscles in his back legs tense. She wasn't prepared when those legs exploded upwards, pushing through the canopy of the trees. The whoosh of broad wings opening to beat violently at the air finally drew her lids back. When she looked, all she saw was the vast starry expanse of night. Nothing above her. Nothing below her.

Mara screamed.

CHAPTER 4

GANNON

IF GANNON HAD COMPLETE control over his body, he would have dropped the woman more than once. Gods, what was with all the screaming? They were scarcely above the canopy. Any attempt at stealth was useless at this point.

So, he climbed higher into the sky, riding a brisk northern wind and letting his wings stretch as far as they pleased. It wasn't often that he allowed himself the freedom to fly like this. Though his presence in the Blackwood deterred most, there were still far too many unscrupulous men on the hunt for opportunity. There was no greater opportunity than discovering where a dragon nested and seeking to slay him for fame and glory.

Men were greedy, simple-minded creatures. It was not so long ago that dragons were revered by the people of Svalta. Gannon's family protected the people of Dunhill and prevented war on more than one occasion. The memories of men were short, however, and already they had forgotten the true nature of the Blackwood beasts.

That was why there were no longer dragon brides, why so many dragons dispersed and sought territory further and further from their brothers. To take a wife was no uncomplicated matter for *drakonmein*. Only one woman would do, and no dowry or political gain could change that.

Utterly unfair of the Gods to build them that way, in Gannon's opinion. The odds of finding the right woman were already astronomical in an ever-expanding world. What if she were to die before their paths ever crossed? What if her heart was made of stone and she betrayed her mate before they were properly bound?

Gannon experienced the answers to many of those questions firsthand. He knew the chances of spending an eternity in misery were far greater than the sons of *drakonmein* were led to believe.

As the estate came into view, Gannon realized that his companion had grown unsettling quiet and still. He'd never carried a person while flying before. Could he have hurt her? Would he land to find the poor woman bleeding out from deep lacerations caused by his careless claws? Gods, he truly was a monster. His dragon had sunk so deep into madness that he was behaving like one of the beasts from the nightmarish tales about maiden-stealing dragons.

No matter this woman's reason for being in his forest, he had no right to take her. If she was fortunate enough to survive her encounter with the Blackwood Beast, she would be returned whence she came.

Unlike Gannon, his dragon was quite confident that the woman in his clutches was fine. He cradled her with such reverence, careful of the pressure he placed on her delicate body. It seemed the dragon was justified in his confidence. The woman shifted, her arms wrapping tightly around his wrist. Her heartbeat was a faint noise over the rushing of wind and wings, but it was there.

She was oddly calm for someone abducted by a dragon.

Perhaps it was her intention to encounter him. Being of the fairer sex did not clear her of suspicion. Anyone and everyone was a risk to a *drakonmein*. If it wasn't his identity they were after, it was his hide. Perhaps she was bold enough to believe she could slay him and earn herself a hefty reward.

He circled the estate's expansive garden, his lip curled back in a vicious smile. No woman would find him vulnerable again.

◆

*M**ARA*
Mara stumbled forward, her knees crunching painfully on the gravel path that came rushing toward her as the dragon all but dropped her. She covered her face with her arms, anticipating the finishing burst of flame that would cook her into a medium-rare delight. That hot, hissing breath was so close she could feel it moving the fabric of her dress. Leathery wings beat once, twice. Gravel shifted under clawed feet.

Come on. She begged. *I can't bear the fear a moment longer.*

In a reckless burst of energy, Mara leaped from her crouched position, taking off in the opposite direction of where she heard the dragon. She tripped over the skirts of her dress several times before she gained any momentum. It was quickly stopped when her already bruised knees crashed into a stone wall lining the bottom of a beautifully trimmed hedge maze.

Mara careened to the right, hoping the maze was narrow enough that the dragon couldn't follow. Assuming he didn't simply melt the hedges with fire. She had to hold her breath to keep the tears at bay, pain pulsing from the abused joints in her legs. Wetness was clinging to the shredded remains of her skirts. Blood, she thought.

Another right, then left, then two more rights, and Mara was hopelessly lost. The hedges were the exact height necessary to keep her from seeing her surroundings and the perfect thickness to block the sounds of a stealthy, hunting dragon. When she paused to catch her breath, the faint crackling of gravel on scaly feet echoed around her. It was impossible to tell how close it was or which direction it was coming from.

She urged herself forward, the hunger to live growing steadily until each bootstep became courageous. Every maze had a way out, just as every prison had an escape. She'd already broken free of one cage tonight. There would be no stopping her from making it out of this maze alive.

That courage faltered briefly when the looming towers of a great stone estate suddenly came into view. The stone was dark, nearly blending into the night sky. Each tower ended in sharp points, appearing like swords thrust to the heavens. Below the towers, black iron balustrades surrounded a balcony that wrapped around the entire upper half of the manse. To Mara, they looked like iron hands creeping out from the stone, ready to curl around anyone foolish enough to walk on their open palms.

The momentary distraction cost Mara her life. A violent roar shook the earth a heartbeat before the dragon burst through the nearest hedge. Except, it wasn't a dragon at all. A massive man with black hair, black eyes, and a face formed of shadows was charging her, muscled arms outstretched. His unbridled fury was startling, though not nearly as startling as his nakedness.

She'd escaped one beast, only to be caught by another.

Mara's cowering did nothing to protect her from her approaching attacker. One thick hand circled her throat, the other gripping her ribs to lift her until her feet were dangling above the ground. Her back smashed into a hedge, and she wheezed. No amount of clawing and kicking could loosen his hold. His grip was iron, as strong and unbreakable as the balustrade hands above them.

"Please," she choked out, unsure if she struggled to breathe because of the hand at her throat or the fear that was flattening her lungs.

It was fear she realized when she turned her head away from the man and found her neck was free to move. The hold was a threat, not a murder attempt.

"Have you come here to kill me?" he snarled, baring his teeth the way an animal would. The words were followed with an odd shudder, and the man shook his head madly, his fingers flexing around her throat.

Mara mouthed the word "no," unable to give life to her voice.

"What were you doing in the Blackwood?" How was it possible that his words came out so jagged? It was as if a bear was speaking to her, not a man.

"Black," she rattled. "Baron Black."

"I am he."

Her eyes opened so wide that she worried they would escape her lids and roll away. This *madman* was the Baron? This was the man King Burne thought would help her. Perhaps their "help" truly was a plot to send her to her demise. The Baron was clearly insane, possibly homicidal. No wonder he hadn't made an appearance before the court in a decade.

Desperate, Mara whispered, "King Burne..."

"Burne?" Recognition flashed in his eyes, making a hint of green appear within those inky depths.

"King Burne Braxenstone of Calos." Tears spilled over onto her cheeks. Why couldn't she have been satisfied with the life she was given? If she were lucky, Lord Wyman would be kind. Gentle enough in their marriage bed. At least he wouldn't punish her the way her stepmother had. Probably. Tomorrow, Mara was supposed to wed. Instead, she would be dead before the sun rose. "He said you could...help."

Those meaty hands dropped from her so fast that she dropped too. The heel of her boot landed awkwardly on the gravel path, sending her toppling to her knees *again*. Mara couldn't swallow her whimper of pain.

Something astonishing happened to the Baron's face. Nostrils flaring, his eyes traveled to her legs. Blood stained the lovely cream where her knees—and half a hundred other places pierced by thorns—were steadily leaking. Not that a stain would make a difference between the dress being salvageable or not. It was an oversized rag now.

As Baron Black looked upon her wounds, his face untwisted from its mask of hatred into a softness that she suspected was uncharacteristic of him. Those black eyes, deeply set into his brow, shifted to a luminescent green. In the dim light of the stars, his pupils appeared narrow and vertical. His expression was concern touched with a hint of adoration. With his broad cheekbones and fiercely angular jaw, he should have looked hard. Mean. Colder than stone.

Somehow, Mara saw none of those attributes. For a heartbeat, she was absolutely certain that she was safe. Whatever troubles followed her, whatever ailed her weary heart, he could remedy it. The Baron was her savior. He would protect her from all of it.

Then without another word, he left. Naked as the day he was born, Baron Black turned on his heel and stomped off into the shadows, leaving her with nothing but the view of his muscular backside as he retreated.

Gods have mercy. What was happening to her?

CHAPTER 5

MARA

MARA ALLOWED HERSELF TO respond to her harrowing night the way she did after one of her stepmother's punishments. For two minutes, she sobbed out her anguish, panic and frustration spilling out in salty tears. Then she wiped her cheeks, brushed black curls from her face, and straightened. There could very well still be a dragon out there with her—unless the Baron scared him off, which was plausible given his ferocious manner—and she wasn't going to get caught again after narrowly escaping.

Her gaze traveled to the monstrous house before her. Black Estate, indeed. The architect must have been in mourning when he designed the place. The entire building was colored for a funeral. Perhaps the furnishings offered more charm than the functional outer decor.

And even if they were as stony and unwelcoming as Baron Black himself, Mara would brave them. She didn't have any other choice. It was the estate or facing the Blackwood once more. Fate had been tempted enough this night with her first journey into the treacherous forest. No use chasing her own demise out of stubbornness.

The Baron might be paranoid and insane, but he still adhered to the law of the land, as far as she could tell. His taxes were always paid on time, and he wrote seasonal reports to the court. The messenger that came from Black Estate was always well-dressed. He gave no appearance that he served under a madman. In his duties, at least, the Baron was sound.

And duty would bind him to treat her as a guest under his roof for the night. Duty would also bind him to return her to her betrothed, but there was nothing she could do about that now. King Burne must have misread his old friend, or perhaps remembered a younger, more lucid version of him. A baron who stormed naked through his own gardens in the middle of the night and attacked helpless women with accusations of assassination was not likely to be sympathetic to a wayward bride.

He wasn't likely to be sympathetic to anyone.

Chin up, because pride felt as if it was all she had to hold herself upright in that moment, Mara began a careful march in the direction she watched the Baron retreat. If she'd been thinking on her feet, she would have followed him and saved herself a series of wrong turns. The upside of having her gown shredded was that she now had the perfect fabric to use as markers. Each time she made a turn, she ripped a strip from her skirts and tied it to the corner of the hedge, preventing herself from going in circles.

By the time she found the exit, she was wobbling on her feet. The inner slip of her dress was sticking to the drying blood on her knees. Those aforementioned knees throbbed, and just about every other part of her ached as well. Only the fading adrenaline that spiked when she reminded herself of the dragon kept her moving. She was hobbling to the back of the house, eyes fixed on what appeared to be a kitchen door, when it opened.

From the outside, the manse looked devoid of life. There were no candles flickering behind windows, no shapes moving around beyond closed drapes. Yet when the door swung wide, a blinding yellow glow washed over her, forcing her to cover her face.

"My lady!" A woman's voice called out to her. Only a heartbeat later, a woman's hands were grabbing her forearms to steady her. Though they were small, those hands felt firm and rough. A working woman's hands. "Gods, child, what happened to you?"

"Dragon..." Mara murmured, uncovering her face to look upon her savior. The woman wore the plain-colored garb of a servant, a light brown that matched her complexion. Her eyes were a shade darker than the rest—a beautiful chestnut, alight with kindness.

"Please, may I enter this home as your guest?" Custom dictated that she was to ask the master of the house in order to receive the security offered to guests by law, but she wasn't keen on speaking to the Baron again so soon.

"Dragon? *He* did this to you?" Mara had never heard a woman more incensed, except maybe her stepmother during one of her fits. "I'll skin that slippery bastard myself. Gods, such cruelty is unacceptable. Nigel! Come quick!" Those kind hands moved from her forearms to her shoulders, guiding her to the open kitchen door. "What's your name, girl?"

"Mara—" She hesitated, swallowing down her father's surname lest she give herself away. "Mara."

Mara got the feeling those chestnut eyes could see all the way into her soul. The kind woman noted the hesitation and nodded briefly. She couldn't have lived more than twenty and some years, but the deep understanding etched into the fine lines of her face made her look ancient. Whoever she was, this woman was an ally.

"Pleased to meet you, Mara. I'm Elsie." Even in her filthy state, Mara must have resembled a girl of her station. Otherwise, Elsie was being exceptionally polite to a dirty beggar.

A stout man in a soiled apron charged into the night, rolling pin raised high above him as if he expected to beat back the dragon with it. His head was bald but for a halo of hair. The missing middle section must have migrated down his skull to sit beneath his chin. Several curses Mara hadn't had the pleasure of hearing before left his mouth when he got a good look at her.

"The *dragon* did this to her." Elsie said, not an ounce of fear in her words.

"He wouldn't." Nigel shook his head, though it was less a true denial and more disappointed resignation. Both parties sounded as if they were ready to hunt the dragon down and scold him. Perhaps living so close to the Blackwood had alleviated their fear of the beast.

"Poor creature. Come inside. We'll get you right." Under his breath, he added, "Cruel bastard ought to be ashamed of himself."

Mara followed numbly as she was led through a massive kitchen and seated at a servants' table. Bags of flour were stacked neatly behind her, and root vegetables hung from various places on the wall. It was the tidiest kitchen she'd ever seen, which was likely because there were no staff in it but for the two in front of her. A lone pot bubbled on the stove, filling the air with a delicious vapor that reminded her she hadn't eaten since breaking her fast.

"Where...where is everyone?"

"Everyone who?" Elsie asked, fetching a bucket of water and a rag from the far corner of the room.

"Your kitchen staff. Have they retired for the night?"

"You're lookin' at the kitchen staff, my lady." Nigel roughed up his beard.

"And the cleaning staff."

"Groundskeepers."

"Personal servants."

"Glorified privy cleaners." Grumbled Nigel.

Elsie tutted. "Don't be foul, Nigel. You and I both know Edgar is the only one willing to deal with that mess."

"There are only three of you?" Mara's mouth hung ajar. "To manage this entire estate."

"Indeed." The word left Elsie in a tired sigh. "Most of it is unlived in, thus there isn't too much for us to do. The west and north wings are empty, have been since the brothers Black left for the mountains nearly ten years past.

"Did he bite you?" She gestured to the blood on Mara's legs with her chin. "Attack you?"

"No, he didn't hurt me." Now that she thought about it, Mara's injuries were all accidents. That didn't mean the dragon hadn't merely been playing with his food. "I fell. More than once."

"Did you make it all the way here from the Blackwood? On foot?"

"My horse was spooked in the forest. That's when the dragon took me."

Nigel scowled. "Took you?"

"Yes, he flew me here. I was sure he would eat me."

He and Elsie exchanged a strange look. "He do anything else? Anything notable?"

"He sniffed me. Then he chased me into the maze."

"Nigel, why don't you put on a kettle and serve some soup? Lady Mara can eat with us." Elsie carefully lifted the fabric of Mara's dress, working it away from her bloodied knees. "We'll get you cleaned up first, then we'll see about speaking to the Baron."

"I'm sorry to impose. It wasn't my intention to interrupt your meal."

"It wasn't your intention to be stolen by a dragon either. Apologies are not necessary. We haven't hosted guests in years. It'll be good to hear some new voices in this house again." Her hands were deft and efficient, cleaning the dried blood from Mara's skin. She wrung the rag out and did it again and again, repeating her gentle strokes until Mara was blood-free. Her dress, unfortunately, was not going to clean up that easily.

Gods, she didn't have anything else to wear. If only she'd been prepared to leave, stashed a bag in the kitchen or the stable. Though until this morning, she hadn't planned on going anywhere. What a foolish, foolish choice it was to run. Did Queen Sophia really expect Mara to make it to Calos? She scarcely made it to the forest. How was she to get anywhere when the baron discovered who she was?

An hour later, Mara had a full belly and a fresh gown. She hadn't asked Elsie where it came from because it was impolite to inquire about a gift. Based on the shimmering fabric—a shade of blue that was the color she imagined the ocean—the garment wasn't one of Elsie's. The housekeeper's dress was clean and free of tears, but she clearly wore it often. And it was made from something practical and durable, perhaps wool. Mara felt momentary envy. She'd never worn attire that allowed free movement. What did it feel like to bend and stretch without worrying about harming a luxurious gown?

The women of the court would be horrified to see her in anything that wasn't made of silk or crafted by one of the popular dressmakers.

"Through here, my lady." Elsie guided her from the kitchen down a long servant's hall. They emerged in a dark, empty dining room. Only the light of Elsie's lone candle kept Mara from stumbling in the shadowy hall.

They passed a winding staircase, bathed in the pale fingers of firelight trying to escape the parlor. Elsie ducked through the parlor door, and Mara followed obediently, though not before staring at the seemingly endless steps. How many floors did the house have? Mara counted at least four landings.

What was a house this large doing empty? Why had the rest of the Blacks left? Did they not have wives? Children? Anyone? By her math, the youngest black brother was nearly six and ten older than her. Surely a man of such wealth and good breeding wouldn't have trouble finding a bride.

"The baron will be with us momentarily." Elsie set her candle on a polished mahogany table, using it to light the candelabras decorating the walls. "Can I offer you more refreshments? Tea? Wine?"

"I am well, thank you." Mara curtsied lightly. "You are a most gracious host."

"You need not waste those refined manners on me, my lady. I'm only a housekeeper."

You are so much more. Mara wanted to tell her. But it was improper for her to cavort with the staff, and Elsie was probably trying to remind her of that without coming across as chiding. After her vulnerable moment in the kitchen, Mara felt comfortable around the woman. She would do best to keep that to herself.

The last time she was comfortable with a servant, the boy had his hands caned to the point of breaking a finger. He couldn't work for weeks and would go hungry until he pulled his weight. As if he hadn't already been skin and bones to begin with, which was why Mara shared with him.

Her punishment was no less severe, though her stepmother was careful not to leave marks that would be visible above her gown. A black and blue princess was an ugly sight, Lucilla reminded.

Lost in the memory, Mara hadn't heard the stomping footsteps on the staircase. She only noticed the baron had entered the room when Elsie's harsh tone drew her attention to the doorway.

"I've put her in a fresh gown and fed her, but she'll be limping for a week thanks to you."

"I'm not in the mood, Elsie," the baron growled.

"And I wasn't in the mood to clean up a bloody, terrified girl before dinner, but you left me no choice. Do you have any idea what you've done to the poor girl? You *left her* in the maze. How could?"

Mara felt a familiar ice form in her chest. She desperately wanted to intervene, to quiet Elsie before she earned a terrible punishment. The queen would have backhanded a servant for speaking so freely. What would a man like Gannon Black do to Elsie? Mara couldn't stand the woman being hurt for her sake.

"I wasn't thinking clearly."

"No, you were not." Elsie lowered her voice. "You're getting worse."

Gannon shocked Mara out of her panic by saying, "I've been trying to tell you that for months. You stubborn mules may as well go. A good life is out there waiting for you."

What was wrong with him? Was he ill of mind? Was that why he was naked in his garden?

"I will die in this house." Elsie pushed her shoulders back, the embodiment of the aforementioned stubbornness. "Why did he take her?"

"What does that matter?"

Another of those exchanges that had no words, just as she'd done with Nigel in the kitchen. They had secrets they weren't keen to discuss in front of her. "You know it matters."

"I'm not speaking of this with you again!" A touch of that anger from the garden showed in the baron's dark eyes. They weren't black, Mara noticed, but a very dark brown. Murky water. The kind that had frightening creatures swimming under its surface. "What you're hoping for has already come and gone. There is one and only one."

"And what if you had the wrong one? You yourself said that—"

"Do not burden me with words spoken privately, in a moment of weakness, while we have witnesses. You overstep, Elsie."

A loaded moment passed, then Elsie did the unthinkable. She raised her hand and smacked Baron Black right across the face. "That's for leaving her bleeding and alone in the maze, scoundrel." Afterwards she curtsied low, every inch of her the obedient housekeeper. "Do call if you have a need for refreshment, sir."

The baron stood in the doorway, rubbing his cheek and grumbling curses to himself. When his eyes fixed on her, Mara was sure she saw them brighten and become viridescent. She didn't have time to discover if her mind was playing tricks on her as she dropped her own gaze, curtsying low and staying there. Heavy footfalls thudded dully on the carpet until Baron Black's boots came into view.

"Forgive me, sire, for intruding upon your home. It was not my intent to create a scene."

"Yes, well, you've failed. A scene has been caused." A pause, then, "Why are you still bowing?"

"Respectfully, sire, you are above my standing, and I do not wish to insult you as a guest under your roof."

"Who said you're my guest? And you're not below my title. I know you're no peasant girl. Your curtsy is too graceful, and you're too comfortable in that gown. What's your name?"

"Mara."

"Mara who?"

Her legs began to wobble from holding her position for so long. Why wasn't he letting her up? "Mara—" She stumbled to the side, her bruised and bloodied legs refusing to hold their position.

A strong hand wrapped around her upper arm, the same hand that had only an hour ago been about her throat. Mara should be frightened to be alone with him. When he carefully lowered her to the nearest chair, his eyes traveling her form with concern, she found she couldn't muster any fear. That strange feeling of security came over her once more, a calm she desperately wanted to keep.

"Are you alright?" His hands were so warm as they absentmindedly stroked the curve of her arm. "How...how badly are you wounded?" Was that regret on his stern features?

"I-I'm fine. The night has been long and strange."

"For the both of us." He stood, taking up against the fireplace like he was posing for a painting.

Mara let her gaze fall to her lap. "Forgive me."

"Stop with the forgiveness nonsense, will you? Do they raise them all so demurely where you're from? Where *are* you from? Your accent is of Dunhill."

"Indeed, I am from Dunhill."

When she didn't say more, he prodded, "Where exactly in Dunhill? What is your family name?"

Voice quavering, she answered, "I prefer not to say."

"Why?" The word was as sharp and angular as his face, making her jump. "See?" He muttered. "She's weak. A scared mouse. Free your head of this ridiculous notion. She's not the right one." All that muttering was followed by an angry growl and a vicious shake of his head.

He truly was mad.

"Please, I only need one night of hospitality."

"And then what?" Those dark eyes snapped to her, burning and intense. "Will you venture back into the Blackwood? Take the road to Calos? That's where you're headed, isn't it?"

"Yes, sire."

A painful quiet drifted between them. Mara practiced perfect princess posture, eyes down, spine straight, hands not fidgeting even though she wanted to squirm under his scrutiny. "How do you know Burne? Are you...well acquainted?" He struggled with the second question, his teeth showing as his lips curled back. His expressions were predatory and fierce. They unsettled her as much as his attention.

"No, sire." She swallowed the saliva collecting on the back of her tongue as a queasy distress climbed up her throat.

"Is that all you can say?" He snapped.

"N-no, sire." She pursed her lips and quickly added, "I am not well acquainted with him. I only met him this morning." Mara explained how Queen Sophia's brother, the heir to the throne of Calos, was killed while trying to slay the dragon. Sophia stepped in and tamed the monster—though none understood exactly how—and claimed the throne as her own. She wed her betrothed not long after, and both were crowned rulers of Calos. "They have scarcely been wed two months. Perhaps their letter hasn't reached you yet?"

"And yet, he sent you to me. Why? If he has reclaimed his family's throne and become king, what was he doing divulging friendships from a childhood long past to you, Mara-with-no-name?" The baron wore suspicion as if it were a weighty cloak.

Mara vacillated between telling the full banquet of who she was and why she was there and offering a mere serving of honesty. After being snatched by a dragon, attacked by an angry, naked Baron, then interrogated by the same man as if he hadn't gone momentarily mad, was an excellent way for a woman to have her eyes opened.

The world outside the castle walls was far more frightening and unpredictable than she anticipated. Was freedom truly worth all the trials? The danger? The fear? She could be comfortable, an obedient wife and a mother to children with good futures. No dragons would stalk her in the darkness. If she was lucky, no hands would be raised to harm her. Or, at the very least, not as frequently as her stepmother's punishments.

Wind carried her as a river current carried the scattered leaves of autumn in her mind's eye, the memory of flying so vivid that she knew she would relive it for the rest of her days. It was a once in a lifetime joy, to be weightless and airborne, for she was not a bird and would never be, no matter how free she became. Yet, she would not have that inspiring memory if not for her bid for freedom.

Another thought occurred to her. Would she have that same liberty in Calos? If, by some miracle, she arrived in Calos to serve beside Queen Sophia, would she become just another pretty trophy? Entertaining guests, the queen had no time for or interest in? Tending to social events by choosing the fabric for tablecloths? Mara hadn't thought to ask. She'd merely darted for the stables and not looked over her shoulder once.

Foolish. Foolish idiot wrapped up in the dreams of a stupid girl. You're lucky to be alive. You'll be lucky if any husband will have you after what you've done.

Some kind of apology was meant to leave her mouth, some quietly murmured explanation and polite request to be returned to her home on the morrow. Instead, she exclaimed, "I will not be a trophy!"

"Come again?"

Her confidence deflated as quickly as it had come. "I-I do not want to be a pretty trophy."

Baron Black rolled his eyes. "And who do you think I am? A trophy maker?"

"King Burne sent me to you, but it was not his idea. Queen Sophia spoke with me. Inspired dreams of freedom within me, and I ran away." *No fidgeting*, Mara reminded her wayward hands as they reached for an invisible thread to pick at on her dress. "From my betrothed. Tomorrow is my wedding day. I am a bride escaped."

He stared at her blankly. No emotion showed anywhere but those eyes. They couldn't hide the storm brewing in that ever-changing color. The implications of her arrival on his doorstep—well, in his garden, actually—were playing out in his head. He was going to send her back.

"Please, sire. I meant to bring no trouble to your home. I only wish…"

"What do you wish for?" The question came with a sudden earnestness.

Her answer rang through the study loud as a bell. "Freedom."

"Aye, I wish for freedom as well."

Mara took in the surroundings, remembered the vast garden and the forest beyond. Overhead, the sky was an endless canvas of light. To her, that was the epitome of freedom. "Do you not feel free here, in this grand home, with a great expanse of wildness all around?" His head snapped to her, and she ducked hers, whispering an urgent apology. "My lord, forgive me. It was not my place to speak."

"I am forever imprisoned, chained within the confines of my own skull. Misery will hold me captive for an eternity until I either grow mad or lose what little will I have left in me." He paced before the fire, teeth gnashing so loudly Mara heard them. "Don't think because you've jaunted through the Blackwood and come out in one piece that you know about freedom."

Mara had no response. It was the truth, but she could hardly be blamed for her naivety. How was a woman to know anything of the world when she was barred from experiencing it?

"All beside the point, isn't it, *Princess Mara*?"

Her heart clambered noisily into her throat. The baron was going to send her back. It was plain on his face. King Burne miscalculated the kindness—and mental stability—of his former friend. A wildness overtook Mara then, as if an animal were thrashing beneath her skin. The need to escape was as vital as the need for air. She couldn't go back. She couldn't be a dove in a cage any longer.

"Don't do what you're thinking of doing."

"S-Sire?" Her legs shook with that violent urge to flee.

"Trust me, you do not want to run from me."

The blood drained from Mara's knuckles as she clenched the skirt of her dress. Any harder and it would tear. "I cannot go back."

"And why is that? Do you find your groom so unsightly? Do you love another?" More pacing, more of that vicious, growling temper.

"He is comely enough."

Again, his irises appeared like churning water, washing between shades of black and green. They were eerily bright in the dim study. "Then there is another in your heart?"

"No, sire. I do not love another."

That stopped his erratic movement. The unnatural stillness that followed was worse. "Why then do you shirk your duty as princess of Dunhill? Is it not a princess' dream to become a pretty bride to a powerful suitor?"

"No, my lord. It is not my dream."

"You dream only of freedom. Is that it?"

"Yes."

"Tell me, what would you do with this *freedom* you hold with such high regard?"

In a rush of bravery, Mara lifted her chin and met him as if they were equals. A terrible breach of polite conduct and hopefully one she would not pay for with her flesh. "Choose. I would choose for myself.

What to eat, what to wear, who to love—the choices would belong to me."

"You and I don't live in a world where we have the luxury of choice."

"Indeed." Her head returned to its lowered state, but in quiet defiance she told herself, "But we could."

The baron gave her his back, gazing down into the fire as he told her, "Your innocence reminds me of myself. If only I had someone to speak sense to me then. Perhaps my life would have unfolded more neatly." She tensed, knowing exactly what he was going to say next. "You have sanctuary in my home tonight. Tomorrow, you shall be returned...to...your...betrothed."

Mara donned her mask of grace and etiquette. "I thank you for your hospitality, my lord."

Where should have been fear and fury was nothing but numbness. The Gods were toying with her, dangling freedom before her as a carrot before a mule only to snatch it away when her teeth nearly reached it. A softer woman would have been in tears. Mara taught herself long ago to shutter that sort of emotion. The pain was worse if you felt undeserving of it, if you wallowed and pitied yourself.

Baron Black was right. She did not live in a world where she was granted the luxury of choice. From the moment she was born of her mother's womb and announced as a girl child, her future was set in stone, carved as deeply as the scars etched into the softest portions of her flesh.

Mara curtsied low and long in the doorway. "I must once again give you my gratitude for your hospitality and for taking an audience with me."

"Elsie will see you to a room."

"I bid you goodnight, sire." This time, she didn't wait for him to let her up before she ended her curtsy and followed the maze of halls and doorways back to the kitchen.

Chapter 6

Gannon

The Beast of the Blackwood. That was what they called him, and for good reason. Gannon was a monster. Truly, down to his marrow, monstrous. Heartless. Broken.

A man broken was a desperate, dangerous creature. A broken man with a dragon inside of him needed to be eliminated. There was no other safe course for him. He knew this time would come. In his heart, he felt the days of his life ticking away, the madness setting in as the dragon grew ever restless, insisting on a mate that didn't exist.

She exists. The beast was insistent. *She is within my grasp.*

Clearly, it was too late for him.

Madeline was out in the world somewhere, probably in the bed of another man, and that knowledge fractured him. Perhaps that was why his dragon was suddenly so intent on that mouse of a maiden venturing down the hall. She was easy prey. Pretty, naïve, hopeless. She was much too fragile for a *drakonmein*, even if he were in his right mind.

She's too weak for you. Gannon goaded the beast that was too alive inside of him.

She is soft where I am hard. No doubt she was soft. And from the moment he touched her back in the garden, there were parts of him that had become unyieldingly hard.

That couldn't be helped. Heartbroken or not, he was still a man. Men had needs. It was a want explained away by biology. Men were as much animals as the rest of the four legged and clawed beings that roamed the forests and fields. The drive to procreate was given to all children of the Gods.

And she smelled fantastic. Gannon had never found a *scent* arousing before, but there was a first time for everything. Roses were his favorite flower, elegant and fragrant. Mara reminded him of a freshly bloomed rose. Soft, velvet petals colored with a beautiful pink blush. He was curious to know every velvety, blushing part of her.

No, he wasn't. That would be a betrayal. Even to think it was wrong. His mate might not have accepted him, but he would wrong her not even in his mind. The dragon raged beneath his skin, becoming a burning itch. He wanted to escape Gannon's control, to push out of his small human body and become the beast once more. That was happening with growing frequency; the dragon demanding to be out, despite having spent most of the night roaming the Blackwood unhindered.

Gannon knew it was a sign that he would soon be unsafe. The dragon unchecked by the man was nothing but a primal creature that eagerly fulfilled its baser urges. If he were to change now, the dragon would make his way up to the second floor, where Elsie had hastily prepared a guest room. There he would find Mara, slipping from her borrowed gown into sleep attire. Her scent would bloom even stronger when he approached her and—

And the thought abruptly ended with a frustrated hiss. That was the greatest pitfall of *drakonmein*. There were no female counterparts to make their match. Any girl children born of *drakonmein* were no different than girls born of an ordinary man. It was only sons that inherited the beast beneath their skin. Thus, the man half of *drakon-*

mein was required for a mating. Hence his dragon's frustration. It was obvious that Gannon was not going to pursue his mate as he should.

He'd wasted more than a year courting some unchaste woman that wanted nothing more than his title and money, only to be *shocked* when she double-crossed him, and now, he was refusing—

"Enough!" Gannon bellowed into the fireplace, smoke puffing from his mouth.

This was how a man went mad. Two halves of himself were at war, his brain an innocent bystander that was quickly losing track of the score. It was time to call his brothers home. They would have to do something about him before it was too late.

"My lord?" Elsie waited in the doorway, for once following social protocol and addressing him properly.

"You must learn to behave yourself in front of company, Elsie."

"Perhaps I will." She tapped her chin, feigning deep thought. "When you learn to do the same."

"I was adequately polite."

"We shall agree to disagree."

"Did you need something?"

Elsie chuckled. "Aren't I supposed to ask you that question, sire?"

Damn Eoin. Elsie was his brother's doing. He brought her here, a frail and frightened thing, years ago, only to leave her care up to Gannon when he decided to retreat to the mountains and become a soldier. Though her appearance was the kind to wrench hearts when she arrived, Elsie was not a delicate flower of a woman. Gannon liked her despite himself.

"Meddling maid." He muttered. "What do you want, woman?"

As always, she cut to the point. "She wouldn't allow me to dress her for bed."

"What do I care? Let her sleep in that gown. I don't know where you found it, anyway."

"I wouldn't allow another to dress me, either." That got his attention. Elsie refused to divulge her past, but it was plain to whoever saw her when she arrived ten years ago, barely a woman grown, that she faced severe abuse. It was Nigel who quietly informed Gannon of the bruises the girl bore.

"I managed to convince her." Of course, she did.

"Is she harmed?"

"Besides what you did?" She cocked her hip into the doorjamb. "Not recently. Likely within a fortnight."

"*Within a fortnight*?" He knew his eyes became the color of his dragon, the world shifting around him as his pupils became little more than slits.

"That right there is why I suggest you re-examine your past." As an afterthought, Elsie added, "My lord."

"What are you talking about?"

"That witch was never right for you."

"Tread carefully, Elsie. My patience grows dangerously thin." He growled back. "Was it him? Her betrothed?"

Elsie leveled her dark eyes on him. "You don't ask a woman about her scars. Ever." On instinct his gaze traveled to the faint line just above her cheek. Contrasting with her warm brown skin, the scar looked white as moonlight. Indeed, Gannon never dared inquire about that mark, nor any of the others.

Scars? Meaning Mara had a history of violence carved into her flesh.

His hand came over his face, scrubbing back the rage that so easily came to him these days. "How many?"

"I overhead you call her princess. Is that who she is?"

"Yes."

"Far, far too many for a girl of her station." Even one was too many, as far as Gannon was concerned. Her gentle flesh should be unmarred by the struggles life thrust upon the meek. "You're not going to let her stay, are you?"

"The law bids me return an errant bride to her family."

Elsie nodded, her tone one of complete understanding. "So that they may punish her as they see fit. Very well. I bid you goodnight, my lord. Do get yourself to bed at a decent hour."

A blind man could see what Elsie was saying with the words she didn't speak. As a baron, he had no say over how a king chose to rule his kingdom or his family. Yet, his greater sense of justice dictated that no man, king or beggar, should be allowed to lay hands upon his daughter. Clearly, Mara was facing abuses at the hands of her family. Was her betrothed equal to her abusers in nature? No wonder she was so keen on escape.

And no wonder she was so very timid. Bravery was trained out of women of high breeding. Boldness too. In Mara's case, he feared that both were beaten out of her.

The swift and sudden urge to climb the stairs, throw open her door, and take her in his arms was unbearable. Truly, denying the instinct made his head throb as if a blacksmith were taking his hammer to it. Gannon found himself taking the steps two at a time, if only to make the pain lessen. He forced himself to a stop just outside one of the many unused bedrooms in the hall that stretched down the south side of the house. Firelight teased the edges of the door, reaching for the darkness in the hall with orange fingers.

Logs hissed and popped as they were devoured by flames. No other noise came from the guest room but Mara's soft breaths. By some miracle, she was already asleep. The even thump of her heartbeat was a soothing balm for his head. For the first time in months—*years*—Gannon fell quiet. Internally quiet. He and his beast were no longer at odds, both taking in the peaceful murmur of Mara's sleep.

I suggest you re-examine your past. Elsie knew of his kind. As did Nigel and Edgar. The men were third-generation servants to the Black estate. They were as loyal companions as a man could ask for. And Elsie? She would take a sword for the ones she loved. Gannon was one of few fortunate enough to qualify for her affection. He looked to her as he would a sister. Always underfoot, always meddling, always keeping her eyes on him with the best intentions.

Elsie hated Madeline. From the very start, Elsie acted as if Madeline were an assassin come to cut out his heart. Well, she'd been right, hadn't she? Even if the dissection were done only in spirit, the damage was the same. Gannon was scarcely alive. By the time his brothers left here, he wouldn't be. Couldn't be.

A dragon who lost his mate to death would die alongside her. A dragon who lost his mate to betrayal withered away and died alone. Gannon had never heard of a dragon's mate turning on him. The bond between them was too strong.

But he and Madeline never completed their bond. Perhaps that was the problem. For him, the attraction was instant. He lusted after her fiercely. For her, the feelings were fainter, not yet enlivened by the magic that came between dragon and mate when her body took his.

She did want him though. It was plain in that first coy smile she gave him. Madeline was a mere shopgirl. Gannon was in the city of Langshire at his brother's behest, slowly dying of boredom as his brothers admired fine jewels and well-crafted weapons. Then he happened upon Madeline and knew that Lady Fate sent him to the city that day.

Her beauty was that of an angel, eyes a bright blue, hair as golden as the evening sun. The way she moved was seductive, a practiced saunter that drew the eyes to her hips. Gannon was a younger man then, foolish and obvious in his desires. Madeline knew he wanted her from the way his eyes traced her form. What she hadn't known at the time was that he was the Baron Black, having just taken his father's place two years prior.

She was also unaware of the other inheritance his father left him. Madeline was thrilled to learn of his title. Her reaction to his other identity was not so pleasant.

If only her father hadn't been in the mix. It was his wicked ways—his *greed*—that led to his demise. Madeline was a good daughter. She obeyed her father's orders, even as it risked her beloved. Gannon couldn't fault her for that. Nor could he fault her for fleeing. To assume that he would harm her was not unreasonable, given the way he dealt with her father.

In that heated moment, when the now familiar rage consumed him, Gannon hadn't been certain that he wouldn't harm her. Which was wrong. Even a dragon gone mad would tear apart the world before he harmed his mate. He wasn't capable of hurting her, not intentionally.

Gannon hadn't hurt her though, had he? The doubts that were trying to niggle their way into his mind came from his dragon. Poor, lonely creature. Elsie was only fueling the decay of his stability, drawing the wrong conclusions from a situation she saw with clouded vision.

Yes, that was all. A hopeless romantic and a dragon gone insane. Princess Mara of Dunhill was nothing to him but an obligation to be fulfilled.

Gannon repeated that to himself until he was deeply asleep, his knees tucked to his chest, cheek pressed against the guest room door.

CHAPTER 7

MARA

MARA WOKE WITH DREAD perched atop her breast. Its eyes bore into her, and its voice whispered cruel jeers. Rolling to her side and covering her ears with a pillow did nothing to quiet the chants. *Foolish. Reckless. Foolish and reckless.*

And there was no reward for such risks. Today, she would be carted back to the castle and face her father. Her stepmother. Her betrothed. All the courtiers who prepared for a wedding that wouldn't come. Any chance of finding her a good match was gone. Mara went from being the desirable daughter of Dunhill to being unmarriageable in one night. No one wanted a wayward bride.

Was it worse to be scorned by her peers and become an old maid in her father's home? Or to be punished by her stepmother for the shame she brought upon the king? Mara shuddered violently, pulling the blanket up over her head to ward off the sudden chill. There would be no end to the punishment now. She would be at the mercy of her stepmother forever.

At least she returned knowing that she fought for her dream. Mara could cradle that pride secretly, reaching out to it when her punishments became too painful to bear. She tried to break the shackles holding her in place. It was more than she could have hoped for, really.

A loud thump and a groan startled her from her misery. Mara pulled the pillow free from her head and sat up to stare at the door, expecting someone to come stumbling in. Instead, there was a gentle knock and Elsie's voice politely requesting entry.

"Enter, please," Mara called to her.

"Good morning, princess." Ah, so the baron divulged her identity.

"Is everything all right?"

"Of course. Why do you ask?"

"I heard...a noise. It sounded like someone was in pain." A man, more specifically.

"Ah, that was the baron."

Outside her door? "Is he unwell?"

"No, but I imagine he'll be a bit stiff after last night. A hallway does not make a pleasant bed."

"Hallway? He—he slept out there?" Was he so concerned she would run off in the night rather than be returned to her family and face her shame?

The other question must have shown on her face, because Elsie briefly explained, "He was concerned for you. The house is large and empty. He didn't want you to be frightened."

"Oh, that's terribly thoughtful."

"He is capable of thoughtfulness once every century or so. How was your sleep?"

"It was lovely. Thank you, Elsie."

Elsie threw open the heavy drapes with a flourish, revealing the mild autumn sun as it crested the treetops. "You don't need to waste your breath on all that frilly formality. No one else in this house does."

"I—forgive me."

"Dearest princess, what have they done to you in that stuffy castle?"

Terrible things. "I was raised to be a proper lady. Etiquette is of the utmost importance for a princess."

She dismissed Mara with a flick of her hand. "I was raised to be straight-backed and soft-spoken too. It didn't stick." Her index finger tapped her chin. "Perhaps that was why my father beat me..."

Mara gasped, unable to find the proper words to express her horror. The world was unkind to women, whether they be princesses or peasants. So very unkind.

"Oh, don't make that face at me. I'm in one piece now, aren't I? They tried to make me crumble, but I held myself together. I find men who speak with their fists often do so because it makes them feel strong." She scoffed. "There is nothing strong about teaching a girl that the world thinks she doesn't matter. Anyway, would you like me to bring you some tea before you dress for breakfast?"

"What about women?" Mara blurted; sheet clenched tightly between her fingers.

"What about them?"

"What does it mean when they speak with their fists?" And their switches and canes.

Elsie weighed her with eyes that knew too much. "I think some women want to feel powerful too. Impotence makes both sexes commit awful acts." A hand landed on Mara's shoulder. She gave only one fierce squeeze before saying cheerfully, "Tea will be right up."

"You are too kind."

"Oh, and Mara?" Elsie paused in the doorway. "You let me know if you need anything. *Anything*."

Mara had the feeling that Elsie didn't mean cookies with her tea.

—◦—

T HE DINING HALL WAS cut from the same stone as the rest of the house. Dark green carpet lined the dark wood floors.

Black chairs surrounded a black table. Tall south-facing windows were framed elegantly by green and black drapes. Even the candles in the bronze candelabras that decorated the table were a smoky color. It seemed the Black family took their name to heart when decorating their home.

Mara stood in a rush, curtsying low as the baron stomped into the room. He, too, was dressed for his surname, his silk clothes as black as the chair he slumped into. Elsie must have been playing on a theme when she helped Mara dress. Her gown was the exact shade of forest green that colored the curtains. She and the baron were just living additions to the darkly furnished room.

"Do sit down." Baron Black's already gruff voice was crumbling stone this morning. Beneath his eyes was stained a shade of dull purple. An invisible weight pressed on his shoulders, and he rubbed his forehead as if pain was sprouting behind it.

"Good morning, sire. Are you well? Elsie said—"

"Better not listen to anything that firebrand has to say. You've got enough trouble without her provoking you." The delicate teacup he grabbed looked ridiculously small in his palm.

Mara had been too distracted by her close call with the dragon to truly notice him the night before. Those hands could grip tree trunks. And his arms might be made of them. For a highborn man, his appearance was rugged. Muscled and tall, inky hair out of place as if he frequently ran his hands through it. There was a thin shadow of hair along that angular jaw too. His features were handsome in a jutting, harsh way.

A match for his home, Mara thought. The house was gothic and dark. So was the baron.

Taking her seat, she asked, "Did you sleep well, sire?"

He leveled her with a scrutinizing gaze, as if she were asking him to divulge family secrets rather than fill the awkward quiet with polite conversation. "Well is a relative term."

That didn't give her much to respond to, so she continued with graceful etiquette. "I would like to express my gratitude for your hospitality once more. You have a lovely home."

"Half the damn place is layered in dust and likely falling to pieces. I'd call it haunted before I'd call it lovely." The baron picked up a biscuit and aggressively scraped butter over the top.

"Forgive me, sire—"

"Gannon." His interruption was not hindered by the biscuit halfway in his mouth. "Call me Gannon." Then, mouth still full, he cleared his throat and grudgingly muttered, "Please."

"Of course, sir—Gannon."

"Are you going to watch me eat, or will you break your fast?"

Elsie wasn't kidding about the manners in this household. No wonder his housekeeper found it acceptable to slap him across the face. If the baron set the standards for behavior under his roof, they were not very high.

"I-I...yes. I shall eat. Thank you." Every moment with him made her feel more off-kilter. It wasn't that he frightened her—though his dark eyes were burning holes through her each time he glanced up—so much as he frustrated her. Mara was so carefully contained, poised and proper, and it seemed to irk him more than it soothed him. How was she supposed to respond to that? None of her lessons as a girl prepared her for a man who hated manners. She wouldn't dare lounge lazily in her chair and eat with her fingers the way he did.

Yet, she was tempted. If only to wipe that judgmental sneer from his face. What business did the baron have to judge her? He was unwed and unkempt, living in a household falling to ruin with only three staff members to attend to him. Poor Nigel and Elsie. And the other one too, wherever he was. Baron Black was not a pleasant man to eat breakfast with. She imagined that serving him was misery.

Still, they did seem to be here by choice. A servant was not a slave, and they could seek better employment at any time. Though Mara supposed she would hesitate to pack up and brave the Blackwood alone if she were them. Even in the daylight, it could be treacherous.

Gods, and she'd thought it wise to bareback a steed through those same woods in the thick of night with nothing but her gown and her foolhardy courage. No, she hadn't thought it wise. At the time, Mara knew her imprudence could lead to her demise. She simply hadn't cared.

How different would her life have turned out if that bottomless bravery had lived within her always? Would her stepmother have given up on a girl that was unbreakable in will? Perhaps the punishments would have only become more severe until Mara's body broke instead. What was a strong will to a girl who could scarcely move?

Her fingers traced the rim of her teacup, a bad habit that made Lucilla livid. Back at home, Mara would have earned a strike to her palm for every circle she made with her fingertip. Feeling a sudden rush of daring, she added a second finger, running the edge of the cup until the liquid inside sloshed. If she were to return home a shame and a burden, due for weeks—maybe months—of punishment, then she ought to take her freedom into hand while she could. It was the smallest, most ridiculous act of rebellion, and it felt incredible.

Until she lifted her gaze and found the baron staring her down with those ever-changing eyes. They'd been nearly black when he plopped down at the far end of the table from her. Now, they were incandescent, as if someone had poured green paint into them and it was swirling around his pupils. Though she couldn't quite find his pupil, almost as if it was thinning.

"Forgive me, sire." Mara jerked her hand back, catching the edge of the cup and spilling it across the table. Mortification and fear became an incendiary mixture, combusting inside her until her face and neck were aflame. "I'm so sorry. Please forgive me."

His chair lurched backward. The screech of each leg made her wince and lower her head further. Boots stomped across the long hall, coming into view right beside her chair. Mara squeezed her eyes shut, thrusting her hand out palm up and bracing for the angry lashing. Anticipation always made it worse, and Lucilla knew it. The tenser her body became, the more pain the rod caused as it struck down on her.

Cloth rustled, and the teacup clinked onto its plate. Perhaps he was going to dump the tea on her the way she'd so rudely dumped it on his table. Her stepmother had done that once. It was an accident, Mara insisted wildly, but Lucilla didn't care. Accidents were unacceptable when she was entertaining company, and she would have to learn her lesson at the family table before she embarrassed all of them. The skin on her thighs was mottled from the steaming liquid. Lucilla hadn't stopped with one cup, opting to empty the entire pot onto Mara's lap.

"Please," she begged. "Please be quick." That kind of please would often earn her an extra lash. Hopefully, the baron wasn't as wrathful as her father or Lucilla.

"You've made a fine mess, haven't you? I can only be so quick." He answered gruffly.

Mara risked a sidelong glance and saw his hand not reaching to harm hers but utilizing his napkin to mop up the spilled tea. "No!"

Her cry startled him, and he stumbled back, knocking the cup off its saucer and sending it rolling further down the table. "What's the matter with you?"

"You mustn't do that!" She yanked her own napkin from her lap and quickly began wiping away the liquid. "Please forgive me. I will clean. Please."

"Mara," Gannon scowled at her, and she flinched. "Mara! Stop it." He grabbed her wrists and guided her away from the table.

The trembling in her hands was so bad that the napkin fell from them, smacking wetly onto the carpet. His grip on her was firm but gently. The warmth that came from those rough palms was a balm to her soul, quieting the fear in an instant. Mara tried to get her mind back on track, tried to brace herself for his ire, but some other emotion pushed its way to the forefront.

She was so...*comforted* by his presence. As if he were a crackling fire and she'd been out in the cold for a hundred years. Frost melted away from her joints, softening her, drawing her forward and into him. Gannon draped one arm carefully around her shoulders, stabilizing her until she ceased to shake.

"That's good. Calm yourself." He murmured, thumb soothing tiny circles on her shoulder blade. "It's only a spill."

"I'm sorry." Mara bowed her head, finding his chest close enough for her to breathe in his scent. There was something familiar about it, some niggling sensation that she knew it. She caught a whiff of a sweet spice—wild ginger—and a fainter, earthier note. *Charcoal.*

A jolt of alarm finally penetrated her strange daze, sending her shuffling away from him. Mara knocked her chair with the back of her elbow, sending a second jolt through her. This one was all pain, and it brought her back into reality. "I am so terribly sorry."

Thunderclouds rolled across his face, cutting his irises in half until they were equal parts ocean green and midnight black. The shadow cast by his thick brow only added to the terrifying sight. As did the way his sharp chin protruded as if it might slice a hole in the air.

Two different instincts warred inside of her. At once, Mara had the wild urge to flee, an animal preyed upon by a predator she was no match for. The opposing instinct said to go to him, that the rage roiling around him could be worn as a shield. The baron was a dark and angry man, but he had no intention of hurting her.

For some reason, she remembered him in the garden, when he'd dropped her back to the ground. Though he'd threatened her only a heartbeat earlier, Mara felt unharmed. There was an ancient, painful loneliness burrowed deeply into his soul. She saw it then, felt it as a kindred spirit to her own ache.

"Were you comfortable in your quarters last night?" The question was so jarring that Mara couldn't form an answer, her lips flopping uselessly. "You will let Elsie know what you need in there to feel at home. There are as many blankets and pillows as you require. Books to read if you find yourself wanting for entertainment. Painting supplies too. Somewhere in this decrepit tomb, there are more gowns like that one. I'll have Edgar fetch them."

"W-what?"

"I won't send you to Calos like a beautifully wrapped gift to a foreign monarch until I've sent a letter and received one in return. The Burne I remember was a good, honorable man, but it has been many, many years since I've last seen him. You are the princess of Dunhill, and you could serve an ulterior purpose in his court. You must allow at least a fortnight for my letter to arrive, likely another before he responds." He balled up her napkin and tossed it onto the table.

"Forgive me, sire, I do not understand."

"And I want you to stop with all that fluffy language. I hate to be called sire, and I don't care for etiquette. A waste of time, if you ask me." That hand reached for hers again, hesitated, then dropped back to his side. "I'm Gannon to my staff, and I shall be called Gannon by you as well."

"Gannon," she whispered.

"Louder."

"I shall call you by your given name. Gannon."

He almost—*almost*—smiled. "Good."

Mara stood stupidly beside the table as he stomped back to his side, swigging his coffee down in one go. He was in the doorway, arm braced against it, when he glanced over his shoulder and said, "One more thing, princess. Don't leave the house at night. And whatever you do, don't go into the Blackwood."

"Sire—Gannon. Wait!" She tensed her hands to keep from fidgeting. *A princess does not fidget.* "I don't understand what you're saying."

"You will not be returned to your father, not unless he arrives on my doorstep with a thousand soldiers. No one will know you're here. Or that you are bound for Calos, if that is where you choose to go."

"You won't send me back?" Her heart became a winged creature trying to escape the cage of her ribs.

His final word to her was a vicious growl. "Never."

Mara nearly jumped out of her shoes when he shouted, "Nigel! Get back in the kitchen and start baking those powdery cakes."

Nigel must have been near because his voice echoed when he replied, "The ones with the apple filling?"

"Yes, and the cinnamon."

"I love those."

She could have sworn she heard a smile in the baron's voice. "They are spectacular. Bring a plate of them to Mara when they're done. And make sure she eats her breakfast. I'm off to write a letter."

Then Mara was alone, the sole color in a gothic room. Whatever had happened in the last five minutes, she was fairly certain it was more shocking than an encounter with the Beast of the Blackwood.

CHAPTER 8

GANNON

GANNON DELAYED WRITING A letter to Burne for three weeks. He didn't intend to keep the princess forever. It was only that he didn't know what to say to a childhood friend he hadn't been sure was alive until Mara uttered his name. Asking after his health didn't quite cover it. He was a king now, back on his father's throne. And he was mated and expecting a child with his queen. Gannon ought to congratulate him.

Bitterness wasn't what kept him from finding the words, necessarily. It was melancholy. Burne suffered a great many losses in his life. He deserved to find his mate.

His mate. *Mate.* That was the sole word that would come into his mind, swirling and sinking into the very matter that made up his brain.

All right, if he were honest, there was a touch of selfishness that kept him from sending his request to the King of Calos and it had nothing to do with jealousy. For over a decade, Gannon lived with an unruly dragon inside of him. The beast became more incensed with time, offended by Gannon's every decision since he began courting Madeline.

Revisiting those memories, he did feel an inkling of doubt creeping into his thoughts. Why would his dragon react unkindly when Gannon planned to bond with her? It was the opposite reaction he should have had. He'd always thought it instinct, the beast trying to warn him of Madeline's crook of a father and the betrayal that would ensue. Now he was touched by a sudden clarity and the images of the past didn't quite look right.

That clarity was born of the peace Mara gave his dragon. Poor beast was so besotted by her that he was all but snoring behind Gannon's sternum. Such a decadent peace it was, too. That dragon made so much noise when he was displeased, muddling each and every thought until Gannon was scarcely capable of dressing himself.

So, admittedly, he was procrastinating. If only to savor the short respite before Mara was sent on her way. He didn't enjoy the feeling of using her, however, and had kept his distance as best as he could. Which meant he was hovering out of sight when she dined and sleeping against her door each night.

That behavior was an unfortunate reminder of the other letter he'd been putting off. His actions were not those of a sane man. And his dragon's fixation on the princess could have no good outcome. Dragons tended to be very territorially and as far as Gannon's was concerned, Mara was his.

It was time to call his brothers home. There were matters of estate to be discussed, and Eoin would need to be prepared to become baron when Gannon was gone. And there was the issue of asking his brothers to kill him. None would be pleased with the request, and none would easily agree. Perhaps they would arrive before Mara's departure and see how far gone he was. They were loyal, but they were prudent too. Of the three, he knew Eoin could be relied upon to do what was best. His brother wouldn't risk Elsie's safety, and Elsie was far too stubborn to leave.

With a sigh, Gannon settled behind his father's desk. Though he'd been a baron for years, he never ceased feeling like a boy perched behind the massive piece of mahogany wood. The office always struck him as masculine. Dark wood, sharp edges, quiet, serious conversations murmuring on behind closed doors. His sire was a fierce man, but he did most of his fighting from behind this desk. The sword he wielded was a quill, slicing through parchment as he traded assets and maintained political relations.

On that front, Gannon had failed as Baron Black. Their wealth continued to accumulate, but the estate fell into disarray as staff were scared away by his unhinged behavior. His relations with the courts was all but nonexistent. As baron, Gannon should have sought matches for his brothers, expanding their family's reach with beneficial marriages.

But his kind didn't work that way. His brothers would accept none but their mates and, isolated as they were, it was near impossible to find them. That was why his youngest brothers had opted to leave the estate and travel north to join Eoin in the war camps. There wasn't much fighting to be done now that a treaty was being drawn, but training to be soldiers and assassins was a better way to occupy their time.

The only other option was slumber. None were too keen on that notion.

"What a waste of life!" Davin, the youngest Black, had proclaimed. "I don't want to wake up stiff and hungry, not knowing what year it is or if any of my friends are still alive. Imagine catching up on the history."

So, Gannon, Davin, and Amos had meandered about the house, pretending to fulfill their duties while sneaking out to the woods, usually with a handful of Nigel's cakes. Eoin was off training young men to be soldiers. He was the only Black brother that was worth anything, truly. The rest spent their days like bored boys.

Bored dragons were dangerous dragons, especially when there were three of them and they were all unmated. As they grew older and more restless, it became difficult for his brothers to stay under one roof together. Too much territorial fighting was bound to destroy the house or worse.

Gannon missed it, though. The noise, the roughhousing—the laughter. Gannon couldn't remember the last time he laughed. He *could* remember the last time he truly smiled. It was a private smile, but the lack of audience did not detract from the way it warmed him.

Mara was growing brave enough to explore the house unattended by Elsie. She never went far from the dining hall or the library, but she risked glances in unused rooms, tried handles on closed doors. Gannon would have to be careful to keep her from the west and south wings. They'd been unlived in for so long that he feared the floors were unstable or the rooms infested with rats. Perhaps he ought to send Edgar to survey.

Only yesterday morning did Mara discover the music room. When she was alive, Gannon's mother insisted her sons learn music and art. She filled the house with oddly shaped instruments and easels with every paint color imaginable. Much to her ongoing disappointment, they didn't take well to becoming cultured. It wasn't that he and his brothers didn't try. They simply couldn't handle the droning of the music teacher or the length of time it took to complete a painting. They wanted to be out in the gardens, to comb the Blackwood for sharp sticks to hit each other with. Upturned logs and all the skittering beetles beneath them were far more fascinating than mixing yellow and red to get sunset orange.

Apparently, Mara hadn't been as unruly as a child. The piano was dusty and out of tune, but even off-key, the melody she tapped out was beautiful. Her thin hands were so graceful as they traveled up and down the piano. The instrument seemed to grin at her, pleased to finally have a purpose again. Even as he slid through the shadows of the hall, watching Mara with a stretching smile, he felt an echo of that melancholy that slowly ate at his heart. It was her song, slow and mournful and loaded with words unspoken.

Gannon wondered if she wrote it herself. Each note seemed too poignant to be memorized. Her shoulders bowed into it. As she played, his head was filled with the image of a clipped bird, caged and so overcome with longing for the sky that it was killing her. It wasn't a song so much as it was a lamentation.

He was brought back to the night he carried her home. As she stilled in his clawed hand, hundreds of feet above the ground, he feared he'd killed her. That stillness, he was realizing, came from her speechless awe. Mara was enamored with the sky, deeply in love with the vast openness. More than once she paused in the hall before her door at night, studying the great painting of the northern horizon of Brula. Hues of blue and purple twined with the dusted white of snow-laden clouds, all wrapped neatly around mountain peaks as if the sky were a cloak for the stony giants of old.

What kind of woman was buried under that obedience and etiquette, he wondered? How would she express her passions if joy hadn't been abused out of her?

That was as close as he'd allowed himself to get to the subject of her treatment at her family's hand. And that was part of why Gannon had been avoiding her. Gods, how she trembled in his arms. Over spilled tea! What horrors did the king expose his own daughter to? More than once, Gannon had considered regicide over the past three weeks. He cared not for the throne or the political gain, only for justice to be served for the innocent.

Women were meant to be treasured by their families, regardless of their standing in society. A princess should be the most cherished daughter in the world. What terrible hatred was befalling Svalta that such gentle creatures were treated so poorly?

No, Mara would not be going back to her family. Not ever. And if she didn't go to Calos? Well, maybe she would stay here. It wasn't as if he didn't have the space for her. She would be provided the luxury that she was accustomed to. Perhaps Gannon would even seek out a match for her, someone kind with a good reputation and—

No. No one but me will touch her. Fire burned at his insides. This was the fourth time today that his dragon had become livid. It was also the fourth time Gannon had sat at his desk and considered the future for Mara, quill in hand. Clearly, his dragon was going to be a problem.

Fine, no letter to Burne yet. Gannon would focus on writing to Eoin first. Perhaps he would enlist Edgar's help when writing to Calos. He'd learned to read and write alongside Gannon and his brothers. In fact, he was the most literate and eloquent of them all. At least on paper.

Thirty minutes later, Gannon was leaving his study on absent-minded feet. The letter to Eoin was sealed and ready to be sent. He was to the point, as always. Davin would read it over Eoin's shoulder and call it blunt. Yet, if he'd asked after their health and waxed poetic about the coming of autumn, they'd have rushed home thinking something was the matter.

Unfortunately, something was the matter. Hopefully, his brothers could read between the lines. It wouldn't be right to divulge his whole dilemma on parchment. Anyone could intercept that letter. Perhaps they would think him a madman talking about *his* dragon. Or perhaps a family secret that was protected for centuries would be outed. Again.

Gannon came to an abrupt halt when he saw where his legs had carried him. Rather, where his dragon had carried him. The scent of roses and honey was rich in the air, mingling with baking spices and whatever meat was roasting. Some part of him was appalled to find her in the kitchen. A princess didn't belong at the staff table.

But seated at that table were his oldest and most loyal friends. And they were also the only company Mara would find within the Black estate, unless she sought Gannon out. Not likely. She was frightened of him, best. He couldn't blame her for spending time with his staff any more than he could blame her for being wary of him.

She should be.

If Mara knew how much of his mind was occupied by thoughts of her, knew that his dragon was circling her like a territorial male in rut, knew that he was *sleeping outside her door*, she would run back through the Blackwood and to her home. After what she'd been through, the last thing she deserved was a half-mad *drakonmein* pining for her.

Not that *he* was pining for her. It was all his dragon. Gannon wasn't capable of loving another woman. He was doomed to die alone.

Dramatic coward, his dragon snorted. *You'll only die alone if you keep following her like a pitiful scavenger feasting on the scraps she leaves behind.*

He was at her heel like a hungry fox after a hunter, wasn't he? That could be so easily remedied. He need only sit beside her, slide her from the wooden bench and into his arms. Her lips would be giving when he pressed his to them, her mouth so moist and sweet and—

That was not the voice of his dragon getting carried away with lustful thoughts.

Feeling nonplussed, Gannon was prepared to back out of the kitchen and return to his study. His retreat was foiled by Nigel's booming voice. "Baron Black! Good sir! Have you come for some meat and mead? It's been too long since you supped with us."

"I—" *Quit stammering. You're a baron, not a lovesick boy.* "I came to retrieve the princess. She's a guest in my home and you have her dining in the kitchen? Unacceptable." Wonderful, now he sounded like an absolute ass. The implication that dining with *them* wasn't good enough for Mara would sour the meal for all of them. Gannon could already see the ice forming over their faces.

"The princess was lonely, *sire*," Nigel told him coldly.

"Did she tell you that?"

"She doesn't need to be dining alone, and you were nowhere to be found," Elsie cut in.

"*I* was busy fulfilling my duties as baron and master of this household." He was busy thinking about those duties, at least.

Edgar raised his index finger and tapped it beside his eye, then pointed at the princess. Ah, so he knew precisely what Gannon had truly been up to. Sneak.

"Set the table in the hall. She's dining with me."

Elsie opened her mouth as if to argue, but Nigel quickly said, "Yes, *sire*."

Mara was as he had always seen her in his presence, eyes downcast, and chin ducked. Her posture was demure, her silky black ringlets curtaining much of her face. She was the perfect picture of a poised, obedient woman of stature. As still as a marble sculpture and matching in beauty, too. And yet, there was a spark igniting within her. Brown eyes alight with indignation and offense on his staff's behalf.

Suddenly Gannon found he was hungry after all.

CHAPTER 9

MARA

FOR THE FIRST FEW days, Mara stuck to the rooms that Elsie introduced her to. Though there were no activities for her to do besides eat, sleep, and sit quietly, she didn't dare veer from the routine she knew so well. Be seen, not heard. Always appear put together and never, ever fidget. Nervous habits were unbecoming of a princess. It wouldn't do for her to look deranged and anxious.

So, for days Mara was little more than a statue, posed in one of the overstuffed armchairs in the sitting room at the bottom of the stairs. She ate slowly and without noise in the dining hall. And she was very careful not to spill her tea. She bid Elsie goodnight as the sun dipped below the horizon, regardless of whether she was tired. With careful precision, she combed and braided her hair, washed her face, and cleaned her nails. Then, with no more than a whisper of prayer to the gods—one in the old tongue that she didn't know the exact translation for—she was abed.

And awake.

For hours Mara tossed and turned—gently so as not to cause her hair to frizz. She couldn't say precisely what it was that troubled her. The guilt over running from a man that might have made a perfectly good husband? Or perhaps the fear of being found out by her family and returned to bear the shame of a wayward bride. Inexplicably, her mind kept wandering to the Baron. *Gannon.*

It was his absence that troubled her most. No, it was *all* of him. There was a great deal that didn't make sense to her. Why was his house empty of family and staff? Why was he unwed? His brothers too, by all appearances. How did one of the wealthiest families in Dunhill become so isolated? Baron Black was more of a myth than a man in the courts.

Many believed him to be killed by the Beast of the Blackwood, and the correspondences that arrived by messenger were sent by his ghost. Once Mara heard a whispered rumor that he *was* the Beast of the Blackwood, cursed by a witch to roam the forest as a dragon at nightfall. He devoured his brothers and all of his servants, leaving the estate haunted and crumbling. Of course, Mara knew better than to express her curiosity and thus never inquired about such tales.

She readjusted her head on her pillow after that, uncomfortably aware of the silence that blanketed the house. Save for the creaks and groans of wood settling for the night, there was nothing. It would be silly to believe Gannon a beast. Surely, she would have seen some evidence of that by now.

But it was not unheard of for wealthy men to kill their brothers to guarantee their own inheritance and title. As for his missing staff? They too could be victims if he feared they would report his crimes. The few remaining were clearly loyal. Loyal enough to keep such a secret?

Mara couldn't reconcile the man that cleaned up her spilled tea with his own hand to that image. Baron Black was a prickly, strange fellow, but he wasn't greedy or murderous. Her heart was certain of that.

On cue, there was a familiar series of squeaks outside her door. Light footsteps that couldn't avoid making the old wood floors respond to their weight. That was the only other noise that filled the otherwise hollow house. Just past midnight, they arrived, coming down the hall and freezing somewhere near her door. It was possible that whoever was roaming reached the carpeted stairs and ceased to make a ruckus. Mara had considered that it could be a ghost. Old houses were often haunted, or so she'd heard kitchen girls murmuring once.

She ought to feel afraid, but she couldn't stop remembering Elsie's claim that the baron slept outside her door during that first night. Surely it was a tease, the housekeeper attempting to make her feel more at ease. Why would a man with a household full of luxurious beds and couches of all sizes sleep on the floor? And outside her door, no less.

Absurd or not, his imagined presence comforted her. There was a quality to him that felt kindred to her, as if he understood the ways her heart had suffered. Only after the commotion in the hallway did she manage to find sleep.

The next morning, Mara's routine was interrupted. Completely dismantled, actually. Elsie woke her as usual, throwing open the curtains and demanding an honest answer about her sleep. Mara, of course, gave the politest response she could. The housekeeper glared at her; hands planted on her hips. She was a terribly stubborn woman, that Elsie. After two minutes of wrathful staring, Mara capitulated and admitted that she'd been sleeping dreadfully. Just to confuse matters more than they already were, Elsie smiled brightly and thanked her.

At breakfast time, Elsie took Mara by the hand, practically dragging her through the dining hall and back into the kitchen. She was seated on a rough wooden bench at a table that shared little with the glossy one in the other room. A bowl of oatmeal and a cup of tea were dropped ungraciously in front of her. Silverware was piled haphazardly in the center of the table. Formality, it seemed, was not welcome in the kitchen.

"Good mornin', beauty. You look tired. Shall I give your tea a pick me up?" Nigel winked at her, wiping his hands on his apron before reaching into his back pocket and waggling a small glass bottle full of amber liquid.

"I thank you kindly, but I will decline." Mara had never had more than a glass of wine and wasn't going to try something harder in the kitchen of a baron's house before she'd even had breakfast.

"Stop trying to inebriate the princess, you old drunk. She's here to be fed and entertained." Elsie swatted at the bottle in his hand.

Nigel dodged her, popping the cap and adding a healthy splash to his coffee. "Nothing more entertainin' than a drunk lady, as far as I'm concerned. You want eggs, my lady? Pork? Cookies? Elsie said you liked my butter cookies."

Answer him, you dolt. "Your cookies are excellent, Nigel."

"I'll start you with cookies." He slurped his coffee, wiped his mustache with the back of his hand, and sauntered to the other side of the kitchen. "Then we'll fatten you up with the rest."

Elsie and Nigel were hurrying about the kitchen when a figure stepped through the garden door. He approached Mara on silent feet, tall and thin and so very pale. Even his hair was a shade of white blonde. His hands were raised, mouth moving, but no sound could be heard. For a brief moment, Mara wondered if he was a ghost, perhaps the one squeaking down the hallway outside of her room every night.

Elsie came up beside the pale young man and kissed him on the cheek. Obviously, he was corporeal. A sweet pink flushed his cheeks, and he beamed at her before returning his attention to Mara and moving his hands again.

"Edgar says he found your horse," Elsie explained.

"My horse? How?"

Elsie answered for him. "He's good with animals. Knows how they think." She glanced between Edgar's mouth and hands. "He says he's been luring her closer to the house with apples."

Edgar nodded and smiled genially. He was a fairly young man, his alabaster skin flawless.

"You have my gratitude, sir. Poor creature must have been so frightened."

Elsie snorted with laughter before translating the hand gestures that followed. "He says that oaf of a dragon scares everything away." She frowned and shook her head. "Of course, how rude of me. Mara, this is Edgar. Edgar, this is Princess Mara of Dunhill."

Mara recoiled at her formal name, but she still managed to put on a polite smile and bow her head in greeting. "It's lovely to meet you, Edgar. You must be terribly brave if you face the forest. I saw the Beast of the Blackwood. He's a frightening creature."

"Oaf," Elsie repeated, adding her own mutter of, "Stubborn, grumpy oaf." Perhaps living in such close-proximity to the dragon desensitized them to the dreadful presence.

Edgar took a seat beside her. From his jacket pocket, he pulled out a pen and a small notebook. After a few moments of furious scribbling, he slid the notebook in her direction. *It is my pleasure to make your acquaintance, Your Highness. We are honored to have you at our table. You may not recognize me, but I recognize you. I have seen you in the courts when I deliver taxes and news as a messenger for the baron.*

He was Baron Black's messenger? No wonder word from the baron was always vague. Edgar appeared to be mute. Strange choice for a messenger, Mara thought.

Edgar smiled and took the page back, writing, *It is because of my deficiency that the baron sends me to court. He has little interest in playing their political games and finds it much easier to ignore their pursuits when his messenger can only return home with written word. Courtiers are smarter than to write their secret dealings on paper and send them with a lowly servant.*

"That's actually quite clever." She felt the need to tell him his muteness was not a deficiency, nor was he lowly. But she'd learned her lesson and would bite her tongue.

Biting her tongue, as it turned out, became increasingly difficult as the days passed. Mara blamed Elsie's influence most, but Nigel and Edgar were no better. Each meal she took with them, they dismissed her manners. Sometimes they even mocked them, calling formalities petty and useless.

"You're a woman, not a lapdog. I see no reason for you to sit, stay, and obey. Last I checked, it was women who brought both sexes into the world. We are clearly the superior of the two and not so delicate as men like to pretend." Elsie had a bold way about her that Mara so admired. That particular comment had started an argument between Elsie and Nigel about which gender was stronger and fiercer. Nigel and Elsie were always arguing, especially when Nigel added a pick-me-up to his coffee or tea.

Across the table, Edgar smiled and shook his head, mouthing, *Bullheaded mongrels.*

Mara covered her lips with her fingers, barely stifling inappropriate laughter. She was learning to understand Edgar's hand gestures and getting better at reading lips. Edgar was an entertaining companion. He made up for his lack of voice with an incredible mind. Well-read was not how she would typically describe a servant, but Edgar was an exception. Apparently, he had been educated alongside the Black brothers. Their families were close, and Gannon's mother had insisted Edgar receive proper tutoring.

The more Mara heard about the late Baroness Black, the more she decided she liked the woman.

Edgar made another joke as Elsie threatened to toss a muffin at Nigel's head and Mara lost the battle with her laughter. It was only a tinkle of a sound, but it very well might have been the first time she'd laughed in a decade.

Quiet as it was, her laughter was suddenly the only sound in the kitchen. Elsie and Nigel halted their argument. All three of her companions were staring at the doorway behind her. The rising hairs on the back of Mara's neck told her exactly why they'd gone silent.

Baron Black was standing behind her, his gravelly voice making a harsh statement. He was angry. Mara could feel it reverberating off of him. Why shouldn't he be? She'd broken so many rules by sitting at this table. So improper. For once, she didn't feel fear creep up on her as she realized what she'd done. No, he wouldn't punish her. The spilled tea incident proved that. Perhaps because she was a princess and thus above him in the hierarchy of the court.

Did that mean her new friends would be taking the punishment in her stead? A rush of anger warmed her belly, and she glowered at Gannon in a sidelong glance. Though she'd known them a very short time, Mara felt protective over Elsie, Nigel, and Edgar. They were the first people ever to speak to her plainly. Genuine friends that offered her genuine kindness.

Mara was followed obediently as Elsie brought her back to the dining hall. Her spine was straight as the baron pulled back her chair and seated her at the far end of the table. Ridiculous. Why bother dining with her if they would be sitting so far apart that she would have to shout to speak with him? Assuming he wanted conversation and wasn't simply making up for his absence with good manners.

Ha! She hadn't seen one demonstration of good manners from him.

When the table was set, the candles lit, and the food laid out before them, Mara ushered in her bravery and looked to Gannon. He was staring right back at her, so intently focused. The intensity was enough that she almost lost her nerve.

"It was my fault, sire."

"What have I told you about calling me sire?" He groused, cupping his wine goblet and drinking deeply.

Though her voice shook, Mara met his ever-changing gaze and plainly said, "Don't punish them."

A calculating edge slanted his lips up to one side. That half-smile changed his features from hard to handsome in a heartbeat. She had to exhale a long, steady breath to slow her heart.

"Why shouldn't I? What kind of household am I running if the princess of my kingdom is eating at a servant's table with an obstinate housekeeper, a drunk cook, and a...Gods, I don't even know what Edgar does."

"He tends the horses." She clasped her hands together in her lap to keep from drumming her fingers on her thigh. "Delivers your messages, keeps pests out of the abandoned wings, tends to the orchard..." Her sentence trailed off as she realized that half smile had snagged the other side of his mouth and turned into a grin. "Have I said something funny?"

"I'm only amused by how unpredictable you've proven to be."

Riding the excitement of speaking up for her friends, Mara forked a bite of potatoes and told him, "It's rude to make assumptions about people."

"Ah, so Princess Mara never forms her own conclusions about anyone?"

"If I do, I keep them to myself." She brought her fork to her mouth and then paused. "For example, I've concluded that you are the most unrefined baron that has ever lived, but I've politely bitten my tongue."

Gannon roared with laughter. He actually *laughed* at her brash words. Mara had to press her lips over her fork to suppress a smile. "Tell me how you really feel."

"I'm grateful to be a guest at your table. The food is lovely with company to match."

"Do you sit and stay when they tell you to as well?" More wine, but his plate went untouched. Funny, she'd heard the same question come out of Nigel and Elsie's mouths on several occasions.

"Is the food not to your liking? Perhaps it's because your cook is drunk."

"A few weeks with Elsie and your tongue is honed as a blade. I'll have to be more careful about allowing her around my more sophisticated guests."

Mara's hand stilled halfway through cutting a slice of pork. "Weeks? I've been here for *weeks?*" She hadn't been keeping track. The days passed so quickly when she was dining with Elsie and the rest, wandering the house, and slowly becoming brave enough to venture back into the garden.

He cleared his throat, taking the pitcher of wine and pouring another glass. "Of course. Letters take a long time to travel from here to Calos. The Black estate is as far north as you can go in Dunhill without reaching the mountains."

"How do you send letters? Your messenger is here."

"I, ah, have other means. Edgar delivers them to couriers when necessary."

Suspicion soured her stomach. "You have sent word, haven't you? To Calos?"

"Yes," he answered too quickly. Too sharply. "Burne is a king. You'll understand if corresponding with an old friend isn't his top priority."

"Of course." She mumbled, suddenly too anxious to have an appetite. The longer she was here, the more likely that her family would discover her. The Blackwood was the last place they would have expected her to go—which was the point—but eventually they would send word to the baron. A missing princess would not simply be forgotten within a few weeks. Perhaps they would presume her dead at some point. Not anytime soon.

Would Baron Black give her up if they sent calvary here to search for her? Did her father care enough to risk those men if he believed her to be a wayward bride? Perhaps not. But if he believed her kidnapped—a *stolen* bride—then he would do everything to hunt her down. It hadn't occurred to her as a possibility before. Silly not to consider it. Mara was never ever out of line. Her each and every word was practiced, her posture perfect, her manners impeccable. Why would such an obedient princess bolt from her own wedding?

"Is it not to *your* liking? The food?" Gannon wasn't smiling any longer. "You look ill."

"Forgive me, sire." She answered automatically. "I feel a little faint. Perhaps it is the heat from the fire." The fireplace was at her back, and it *was* warm, though pleasantly so.

"I've lost my appetite." He rose abruptly, his chair screeching backwards and nearly toppling. "Nigel!"

The cook appeared in the doorway a moment later. His eyes first found Mara, scanning her features as if he expected her to be harmed in some way. Only when he saw she was well did he turn to the baron. That lapse in attentiveness did not go unnoticed.

"Something catch your attention?"

"No, *sire*," Nigel looked as if he wanted to roll his eyes but refrained. Barely.

"What have you been baking today?"

"Butter cookies, *sire*."

"Again?" Gannon stroked his chin.

"The princess has taken a liking to them."

Black eyes shifted to her, and as they did, hints of green came alive within them. It had to be a trick of the light. "Has she? Excellent. Bring us a plate. We'll take them with us."

"Where are we going?"

Gannon came around the table, drawing out her chair and answering her question with a question. "Have you seen the gallery yet?"

The hallway creaked and groaned under their feet as they walked past her bedchamber. A familiar tingle lit up her spine, and she glanced at him curiously. One hand held a plate of freshly baked cookies. The other, a candlestick. The baron was masculine in appearance and attire, and the plate of cookies seemed silly in his meaty grasp. It was a frilly white plate with floral filigree decorating the edges. Mara suspected that Elsie had selected that plate on purpose, knowing that Gannon would be the one to carry it.

"Something catch your attention?" He repeated to her, somehow knowing her gaze was on him even as he faced a candelabra on the wall and used his candle to light it.

"No, si—no."

"You can be honest with me. I may lack manners, but I won't bite." For some reason, that made him grin.

"I was only noticing your hands."

"My hands?" he purred, taking a right and leading them down a second hall. Gods, this house was a maze.

"You don't have the hands of a baron."

"Do you observe the hands of many barons?"

Yes, actually, she did. Only because she was expected to keep her eyes lowered when not being addressed and that often meant staring at hands. Courtiers and wealthy merchants had plump, soft hands. If they were trained as swordsmen, it was for show, not practicality, and thus they rarely had the calluses and definition of soldiers.

"Some."

His fingers flexed around the fancy plate. "What's different about my hands?"

"You have a warrior's hands."

"Much to my mother's dismay. She wanted my brothers and I to be cultured, involved in the arts and all that." He pushed open a double door, leaving her in the doorway as he tugged back the drapes before a massive window. Light spilled into the room, illuminating a wall of paintings. "Alas, we were much more suited for swordplay and fist fighting. Amos took to painting better than the rest of us, but his talent was nothing compared to Edgar."

Mara approached the nearest painting. The canvas was small, the colors simple. Someone had attempted a painting of a tree. The basics were there...if she turned her head just so.

"That first row is mine. They're hung in order of our age." Gannon offered her a cookie. There was already one in his mouth and a second helping in his hand. He certainly enjoyed his desserts.

Mara accepted the treat, nibbling delicately. "How old were you when you painted this?"

"Seventeen."

She nearly choked on cookie crumbs. Hiding her surprise, she rushed to the next one, examining it the way one would a fine piece of art. There was a long black ribbon painted against a sloppy sky. By the triangular wings, Mara guessed it was meant to depict the dragon. She glanced at the next one and the one after that. Blotches of color, ill-placed eyeballs on strangely shaped figures.

That one on the end looked like—"Is he stabbing someone?"

Gannon studied the splatters of red. "Yes, that's blood spray. It's a depiction of the Dunhill rebellion." His eyes found her face. They were black again, but no less warm than before. "Do tell me what you think of my work."

"It's…" It happened too suddenly for her to stop it. A soft chortle turned into a giggle, tumbling into full-blown laughter. Peals and peals of laughter, so fierce that she had to clutch her stomach to ease the pain. "Dreadful. They're all dreadful."

"Dreadful?" He clapped one of those rough hands over his heart. "You offend me, princess."

Mara wiped a tear away. "This has got to be the worst art I've ever seen."

"Come now, you haven't looked at my brothers' yet. One of them has to be worse than me."

"No one is worse than you." The tease came so easily, as if she'd always had a heart this light.

Gannon stilled, his head slowly easing in her direction. Not a trick of the light. His eyes had changed from black to a shimmering green. They looked wrong somehow, like they didn't belong on the face of a man. But they were spectacular. So beautiful. And so familiar.

"You should laugh more often. It suits you."

"I would say the same about you and painting, but my manners only stretch so far." She snatched the last cookie from his hand and continued down the wall of paintings. Her air of nonchalance was a facade, her heart pumping so loudly she wondered if the baron was talking, and she hadn't heard over the thunderous organ.

How easily she shed the princess mask. Was that voice of hers so deeply rooted that even the worst of her stepmother's punishment could not quiet it? A few weeks on her own and she was making jabs at a baron. Speaking freely. *Laughing.* Gods, she could never go back.

To return to a world that crippled her soul—and her body—would be as good as death. Wasn't a caged bird merely a ghost? So too, was she under the king and queen. So too would she be in a loveless marriage of opportunity.

"Aren't you clever?" He followed on her heel, watching her clutch her stolen cookie in a death grip. "Are you alright?"

She barely managed to whisper, "Of course." Her heart was going mad for a different reason now.

The paintings on the first wall were as sloppily done as Gannon's. Each a rendition of a natural landscape that appeared to be melting or a collection of fruit that was suffering severe defect. The next wall, however, was splendid. Magnificent. Mara wasn't sure if it was the talent that the artist so obviously possessed or the subject matter that had her so enthralled.

Viridescent eyes glared down at her from the canvas. They were framed by scales of midnight black that shimmered like silk in the light of the full moon overhead. Mara knew from experience that they were made of much tougher stuff than silk. Charcoal-colored wings stretched boldly across the image, hiding much of the Blackwood and the night sky behind them.

"He's so very beautiful." A terrible, lethal beauty.

Gannon purred. Truly, it was the only way to describe the rumbling sound that came from behind her. Mara whirled and found herself meeting the same green eyes from the painting. Impossible. She blinked several times, as did Gannon. By the time her vision refocused, his irises were the black she expected to see. But his brow was tight, and the casual charm was gone, replaced by the harsh features of the Baron Black.

Gannon almost sounded angry when he told her, "The Beast of the Blackwood is dangerous. That's a killer you're admiring."

"But can he help what he is?" She wondered aloud. "To kill is in his nature."

"He's not an ordinary predator. He hunts for sport."

Mara shuddered as she remembered the feeling of being hunted. And yet... "He didn't kill me."

Gannon was suddenly much, much closer to her. He leaned into her, inhaling deeply. His breath rolled back out of him in another of those strange purrs. "You are a different kind of prey."

Mara was overcome with a sudden desire to touch him. The room seemed frigid, Gannon the sole source of heat. She shifted toward him, angling herself so that her chest was aligned with his.

He brought a finger to her cheek, tracing the bone down to her chin. "So very beautiful." What was wrong with his voice? It was two stones grinding together.

Green. His eyes were *green*. The change was startling enough that she stumbled back a step, glancing between him and the painting. "Y-your eyes. How?"

A wall shuttered down over his face, and he pushed away from her. With barely more than a glare over his shoulder, he growled, "Elsie will fetch you. I have duties to attend to."

"Gannon—"

He stopped just outside the room. "I'll send another letter to Calos. You won't have to stay another fortnight."

Then Mara was alone. Bemused, she turned to the painting and traced the side of the dragon's face. Something strange was going on in the Black Estate. Where was all the staff? The Black brothers?

And those eyes. *Those eyes*. Mara would be haunted by those glinting emeralds for as long as she lived.

CHAPTER 10

GANNON

GANNON MANAGED TO KEEP away for three days—three *miserable* days. Truly, his misery during his self-imposed isolation was unmatched by any suffering in his life. The nights were the worst, when he had to grit his teeth and fight his dragon from venturing down the hall and making a nest outside her door. He never would have imagined that sleeping in his own bed could be more uncomfortable than sleeping on the floor.

The restless anxiety that his dragon infused him with was worse even than the pain he was dealt after Madeline's betrayal, which drew the faintest curiosity to his mind. He wasn't arrogant enough to believe he'd been wrong about his mate, but perhaps a dragon could find a new mate if he was rejected by the first one?

Nonsense. It had to be. He knew only what his father had taught him about their kind, but never once was there even a hint of a second mate. To find a mate in one's excessive lifetime—before madness took hold—was considered very lucky indeed. Gannon knew he hadn't earned enough favor with any god to be gifted a second opportunity for a bond.

But what if...what if he could choose another? What if his dragon became enamored with another woman and Gannon courted her properly? No one said that wasn't allowed. Common men married women before falling in love with them all the time.

More nonsense. Gannon was *not* considering this. Mara was a wayward bride, for Gods' sake! She wouldn't want him to court her. And if she did? How would he hide her from the king? Yes, it was only a matter of time before her father's messengers came calling. In fact, Gannon was surprised they hadn't already arrived at his doorstep. Was the Beast of the Blackwood truly that frightening? He'd scarcely been out in the forest in weeks.

And sooner or later, someone was going to notice. He was not unaware of the more unscrupulous—and sometimes downtrodden—people that made their living on the outskirts of the Blackwood. They were always testing the boundaries of his territory, searching for signs of the dragon's presence. Greed and desperation made men bold. If word got out that *the Beast* was not in his lair, the estate would soon be crawling with visitors.

Speaking of visitors, Gannon snatched the letter off his desk that had arrived by courier earlier that morning. The seal belonged to a high-ranking officer in the royal army. Eoin was always prompt in his responses, but he was not always obedient to Gannon's word. A soldier, Eoin told him, served no man but the king. Heart pounding, Gannon broke the seal.

Had his brother written to inform him that they would not be returning from the camps up north? Eoin was wise enough to glean why Gannon wanted his brothers home. Perhaps they wouldn't come, denying him the sacrifice he needed from them.

Gods damn him. Here he was fantasizing about *courting* when he'd only just requested his brothers come home and put an end to him. The mind, he supposed, was always seeking distraction from the inevitability of mortality.

Paper crinkled in his palm as he fisted it. Unfurling the letter, he read it again and then tossed it onto his desk. He should be relieved.

Instead, he was suddenly suffocating by dread. His dragon too was frantic. This was not what the creature wanted. Not at all.

He found the object of his desire taking lunch in the dining hall. Since his outburst in the kitchen, she'd been taking all of her meals there. *Alone.* Nigel was right, Gannon thought as he watched Mara artfully spoon broth from her bowl. The princess was lonely. He got the feeling her life was void of true connection. When was she ever allowed to retreat from the severe expectations her family clearly had of her?

Never. Obviously, she was chained by them.

Belatedly, Gannon remembered the scars Elsie mentioned. How bad were they? How many? Was that why she feared him so those first weeks? One incident of poor etiquette and she expected to be beaten. Rage uncoiled within him, taking the shape of a lethal dragon.

Mara gasped, nearly toppling her soup bowl as she whipped around. It was the loud crack of wood that startled her from her meal. Gannon dropped the chunk of doorway he'd taken out with his iron grip and leaned casually over the fresh hole. "Good afternoon, princess."

She pushed back from the table. "Sire, are you all right?"

"Yes, of course. There was, er, a bug."

"A bug?" Mara recoiled a little.

He dusted off his hands. "Oh, yes. Big one. I'll have to have Edgar check for termites."

An awkward silence passed between them before she asked, "Will you be joining me?"

Was it him or did she look hopeful?"

"I—no."

"I understand." She bowed her head. "I'm sure you have *duties* to attend to."

Ah, a jab at his cowardice. How did he explain to her that he was hiding away for her safety? What happened in the gallery could not happen again. Gannon had never before lost complete control to his dragon, especially not when he was walking as a man. Spending any time alone with her was too much of a risk.

Of course, the next sentence from her mouth was, "If you find yourself with a free moment, do consider joining me in the garden."

"You've barely eaten."

"Your staff must be planning to eat me; they've been fattening me up so. This is the third course. And I've already had cookies." She patted her slender stomach. Gannon followed the motion of those lithe fingers as they flattened the fabric of her gown. Gods, he wanted to be that gown. "Does he only come out at night?"

"What?" He shook his head.

"*The Beast*. No one here seems particularly afraid of him. He dropped me right out there, in the maze. That's practically on your doorstep. Is it because he only comes out at night? That you're not afraid, I mean." She looked so different from the demure girl that huddled in his sitting room weeks ago. Curiosity was alive in her eyes. And something else too. Gannon would almost call her calculating, only the expression was too innocent for that. Determined, then.

Curiosity and determination made for dangerous bedfellows around a man with as many secrets as him.

"Yes, I do believe he prefers the night."

"It makes sense." She brushed her mouth with her napkin and lifted her half-empty bowl from the table. "What with all those black scales. He's practically invisible in the dark."

Gannon was too shocked to speak when she carried her own dish back to the kitchen and stacked it with the others to be washed. Nigel smiled cheekily when he saw Gannon was with her. Edgar raised his hands and made several gestures to her.

"Yes, I will be careful of the dragon." Mara watched studiously as his hands moved again. Gannon narrowed his eyes as she giggled. "No, I don't think smacking a dragon across the nose is a wise idea. He's a touch more dangerous than a misbehaved hound."

A touch more dangerous? I could bring down this entire house. I could slay an army of a thousand men. Dragons were incredibly egotistical creatures.

Gannon glared at Edgar, but he only shrugged and waved Mara off. She was already exiting through the kitchen door when Gannon jogged after her, yelling, "Wait, Mara!"

"Yes, sire?"

She smirked privately when he corrected, "Gannon, please."

"Yes, Gannon?"

"Let me join you." He rubbed his jaw, realizing he was in dire need of a shave. One of the many, many details that slipped his mind as of late. "Just to be safe. The dragon is not the only predator that lurks in the Blackwood."

She nodded with a smile, taking slow steps toward the rose garden. Her head moved on a swivel, looking from the manse that loomed over them to the rose bushes and the trees, both of which were equally bare. There was a variety of rose—his mother's favorite—that bloomed year round, even in the snow, but it was planted in the center of the maze. A reward for anyone who managed to navigate it.

Autumn was in full swing now, the breeze nipping gently but consistently. A carpet of gold and brown covered almost everything within reach of the forest. Apples and pears dropped heavily in the orchard, bringing rodents and other scavengers—sometimes a bear if the creature was feeling particularly brave—to collect what Nigel and

Elsie didn't. With each season that passed, the estate became wilder. An untamed landscape gradually devouring all that was manmade. If he didn't staff the house soon, it would fall into ruin, vines taking hold and animals encroaching where they didn't belong.

A rough gust scattered leaves at their feet, and he shivered, not from the cold but from his next thought. Eoin would have to handle it. As the second oldest, it was his responsibility to man the house once Gannon was gone.

Gone. The finality of that word was so ugly that he forced himself away from it, choosing conversation instead of silence.

"My brothers will be home in a fortnight," he told Mara.

She ran her hands along an empty bird bath, her gaze flitting from the maze entrance to him. She'd been eyeing it since they stepped out. "Are they still up north? Elsie said they were training to be soldiers."

"They are. Eoin is a captain. He fought in the war. Davin and Amos only joined him recently. They grew bored of court politics, I suspect." He angled his body to block the wind from her.

Mara closed her eyes briefly, expression sad. "Have they enlisted? The younger two?"

"I don't believe they have. Not yet, anyway."

"I pray they find another path." Their walk took them in a circle around the west wing of the house. The greenhouse came into view when she turned back and glanced at the maze once more.

"Do you want to walk the maze? You'll be safe. I'll make sure of it."

Hesitantly, Mara nodded, wrapping her hand around the crook of his elbow and pressing into his side. Gannon had to inhale a deep breath before he could think clearly enough to guide them toward the hedges.

She's a beautiful woman. She's a beautiful woman, and I am a man isolated. Of course, she makes my heart race. Any man would be thrilled to have Mara on his arm. And even the thought of it being another with his arm in her hand made him see flames.

She is not your mate. He told his dragon uselessly. The beast was too busy basking in her affection to listen.

Mara tensed when they passed the first row of hedges and took a right, but she didn't slow. Gannon let her lead, impressed that she seemed to remember the way she'd come in. They made a few more turns, and she shivered in the shadow of the maze. He rested his hand over hers.

"You're very warm." She blushed.

Dragons tend to be.

No matter how closely they walked together, it was not close enough. He could think of several better ways to keep her warm.

And that was enough of that.

"Can I ask you something?"

"Yes, of course." Mara ran her fingertips along a hedge, the evergreen leaves rustling.

"Why Calos?" It was the wealthiest neighboring kingdom, but not the closest or the easiest to access. Calos was surrounded on three sides by mountain ranges. The only way in or out of the kingdom was by boat or through a mountain pass that became treacherous for travelers during the winter. If Mara planned to make it there this year, she didn't have much time left before the snow prevented her journey.

Gods, he was rotten. A terrible, rotten man. He could blame the dragon for many of his faults, but not for the letter that sat unsent on his desk.

"Queen Sophia offered me a place there. A new life." Her gaze unfocused, and she slowed. "It was the only opportunity for freedom I'd ever been offered, and when she gave it, I realized how desperately hungry I was for more."

"And your groom was not a man who could give you freedom? Life outside of Dunhill?"

"If I'm being perfectly honest?" She sighed. "I'm not sure. But I knew he would have...expectations. And what if he was hateful? Secretly so, like my stepmother. I couldn't live with a lifetime of bruises and—" Mara shuttered her words so quickly her teeth snapped together. They'd both stopped walking, the air still around them as the wind was blocked by the maze.

"Mara—"

"Please forgive me. I'm speaking too freely. I seem to have forgotten myself." Her hand slipped from his arm, and she palmed her heart. The scent of her panic laced his every breath, and he felt the shift as his eyes began to change from man to dragon.

"Mara, calm down."

"I-I can't." Suddenly she was panting, stumbling backwards.

"It's all right."

"No—I can't go back there."

"Come here, Mara." He couldn't keep the growl from his voice. "Come to me."

She reminded him of an injured bird, so fragile as she huddled against the hedge. At his command, she came forward, hugging herself. Her trembling was not only from the cold, he could tell. Ignoring his better judgment, Gannon took her in his arms, resting his chin atop her head and murmuring reassurance. Deep within his chest, his dragon did the same, vibrating with comfort.

Mara slowly softened into him, her cheek coming to rest on his chest. The smell of her sweetened, becoming honey and rose petals and a peace that overtook her panic.

"You'll never go back. I'll make sure of it."

She burrowed further into his hold, and he allowed it. Didn't only allow it, he begged for it, willing every spark of heat in his body to warm her so that she never felt the urge to leave.

She could stay here always. A tricky little voice murmured. Or was that the voice of his dragon? It was true. Here, so deep in the Black-wood, at the base of the mountains, they were safe from prying eyes. Mara could disappear in the Black estate, and no one would be the wiser. But it would be an escape built on dishonesty, and it wasn't safe for her. Not so long as he was so helplessly fixated on her.

What would his dragon do to get her attention? Not three weeks earlier, he'd been hunting her in this very maze. As if that was the way to woo a woman. Poor sweet Mara didn't deserve the obsessive love of a rejected dragon.

"I'm sorry. I don't know what overcame me." When she pulled away, it was stiffly, as if her body resisted the movement. Her palm rested on his bicep even after she retreated, her gaze finding his and locking onto it with a strange awe.

That was when Gannon remembered what his eyes looked like and quickly turned away. "Shall I show you the center of the maze?"

"Wouldn't that be cheating? I'm sure you know where it is."

He chuckled. "My mother would have loved you. She used to make party guests wander her maze for hours. It didn't help that she would get them drunk first."

"She sounds like enjoyable company."

His answer was bittersweet. "She was."

Mara finally put space between them, dipping her chin. "Can you show me where we were the night I arrived? Where you found me?"

"Ugh, yes. Why would you like to go there?"

Her shrug was too nonchalant. "Curiosity, I suppose."

Gannon pretended to count out his turns, when in reality this path through the maze was seared into his mind. That night he thought he'd permanently lost his mind. Or perhaps his body, as it was nearly impossible not to shift back to the dragon once he walked away from Mara. The beast was enraged, not only at his treatment of her but his dismissal. Gannon had to get out of there, though. The scent of her blood and the innocence in her eyes was too much.

There was a loaded moment where Mara looked to him as if he was a savior. It was such genuine admiration that he felt physically ill. Gannon was no one's savior. He destroyed what was divined by the Gods. Mara was much more fragile than the will of capricious deities.

"I can't save you!" he almost screamed at her. The catch was that he wanted to. It was selfish. Helping her gave him something to cling to, some sanity that felt steady for the first time in years.

Mara approached the hole in the hedge where the beast had burst through it in pursuit of her. She reached a hand out to touch the destroyed foliage, freezing halfway there to cock her head as if she expected the dragon to reappear out of thin air. When no creature of the night came thundering in, she traced the jagged edges of broken twigs.

"My father has a menagerie." Her finger stopped on a leaf. "He has an obsession with keeping exotic animals. He likes the beautiful ones—colorful birds he can show off to guests—but his favorite are the most dangerous. I think caging predators makes him feel powerful."

Gannon rested against the stone wall at the base of the hedges while he listened. "There was a white tiger once. Such a ruthless animal. Even though my father kept him half-starved, he still played with his food when it was given to him. Perhaps because he was so very bored by captivity. Perhaps because that is the nature of predators." She rubbed the leaf between thumb and index finger, gaze scanning the forest now visible beyond the maze. "I imagine that was how the goats felt when he chased them. I knew that dragon wanted to catch me, but I had a feeling he wasn't going to eat me just then."

At all. He definitely did not want to eat you.

"Dragons are...mysterious. Who can say what their nature is?" *Besides me, the dragon.*

Mara flicked her eyes up and then back down to her leaf. "Do you have many enemies, Baron?"

"I have none, that I know of." Unless Madeline was out there plotting revenge. It would be difficult to convince someone that what she knew was true, but the right audience could be dangerous to him and his brothers.

"Then why did you think I was here to kill you?" She smiled a little. "*Me?*"

"Oh, right. That." Gannon scrubbed the back of his neck. "Well..." What reasonable explanation was there for their first meeting?

"And while I'm asking, why were you undressed? Do you frolic about your garden without clothing? I should be more careful to shut my curtains lest my virtue is disturbed."

"You're joking." Who was this beautiful, lighthearted creature he kept getting glimpses of? Someone too humble for a princess, too kind.

"Partially." A small shrug. "I do actually want to know why you...approached me as you did."

"I..." Thinking fast, he blurted the first idea that came to him. "I sleepwalk. My body has a mind of its own. Some nights I'm shocked by where I end up." Not entirely untrue.

"Oh, how terrible. It must be disorienting for you."

"It is."

She was quiet for a time, lips pressed together as if to hold in more questions. Finally, they fought their way out, and she asked, "So it is you? In the hall at night. Elsie said—" Remembering what he said about listening to Elsie, she cut herself off.

Damn, she was far too observant. Gannon needed to get her out of here before she noticed his odd behavior. Even the thought made the winged serpent coiled in his belly strike out. Or was that his own sense of dread? "Probably. I don't always recall what I do in my sleep." *Liar, and a bad one at that.* "Have I frightened you? Such a big and empty house can be intimidating."

"No." Mara turned and started back the way they'd come, avoiding his gaze. "For some reason, I find it comforting." Then, too quietly for an ordinary man to hear, she whispered, "I'm tired of feeling alone."

Those five words resonated so deeply with him that they struck his soul. He too, was tired—so very tired—of being alone. A man was not meant to wither away at his desk, finding no joy to remove him from the weight of his duties. Neither he nor his dragon could live much longer as they had been. It was taking a toll on his heart.

"Will you show me the center of the maze now?"

"I thought you said that was cheating."

Mara smiled over her shoulder. Truly, she was angelic. Her nose was the perfect, delicate shape for her face, her cheeks high but filled out enough not to give her that sharp, gaunt look some courtiers carried. The most stunning feature was her eyes. What were once vacant discs filling her sockets were now bright and alive. Brown could be such an ordinary color, but Mara wore it the way some women wore rubies and diamonds. Sparkling, rare.

"Perhaps you should set me loose and see if I can find it on my own."

"And if you don't?"

Her smile widened. "I do believe you'll have to come rescue me."

"Hmm." He scratched his chin. "I'm not really the heroic type. What will you give me in exchange for my services?"

Her teeth bit down on her plump bottom lip. Gods, she was going to kill him. Was she even aware of how tantalizing she could be? "What do you want?"

You. Preferably naked, my name on your tongue. No. Wrong answer. He had no right to use her as fuel for his fantasies. "A song."

"A song?"

"I heard you playing. You're very good."

She shrugged. "A talented and cultured woman makes a better wife."

"I want you to play something for me."

Mara stared at him for a long moment. Her smile faded, expression becoming searching. A hint of those forlorn lines she wore when she first arrived appeared around her eyes. Then she smiled—that fake, polite smile that he was coming to hate—and said, "As you wish, sire."

CHAPTER 11

MARA

MARA HAD A PROBLEM. Well, if she thought about it, she had many, many problems. This one, though? It was going to leave her devastated if she didn't deal with it promptly. How exactly did one deal with a blooming heart? Did she simply stomp it down like an unwanted weed, crushing the petals and leaving it unable to grow? That seemed so terribly cruel.

And a waste to destroy such a thing of beauty.

But she also couldn't allow herself to continue down the path she had stepped onto during that afternoon in the maze. Baron Black was showing her kindness—more than she thought him capable of when she first arrived in his home—but that didn't mean he had any interest in her beyond aiding a helpless woman. Gods, she must appear such a fool to him. What knowledge did she have of the world, besides what she'd been taught in her studies? What experience did she have outside of stuffy brunches with courtiers?

Besides, it wasn't as if he could take her as a wife. She was a wayward bride—as unmarriageable as an unvirtuous woman, as far as most were concerned—and a missing princess. Her father would never give Mara permission to marry a man of her choosing, especially not after what she'd done.

She was getting ahead of herself. Gannon hadn't been in the same room as her until a few days prior. Why should she entertain daydreams of marriage when the man couldn't be bothered to dine with her?

So pathetic.

And destined for a different life. There was a place waiting for her in Calos. She would become another person, a woman reborn.

Gannon hadn't made an appearance at breakfast or lunch, and he had yet to emerge from his office. Mara was determined not to feel disappointed by his absence. One afternoon of polite company did not make him obligated to spend time with her. A baron didn't need to waste his time entertaining unwanted guests.

Trying not to think of the way he held her yesterday when her panic overtook her, Mara wandered down the stairs, through the hall, and to the music room. She brushed her hand over the piano, pushing herself to forget the way Gannon laughed as he retrieved her from yet another dead end in the maze.

She pressed a key experimentally, the single note echoing hollowly in the empty room. Would he ever ask for the prize he rightfully earned, or was he simply being kind? Mara couldn't bear the thought of waiting another three weeks to see him again. How could he be a ghost in his own home?

Surely the sound of the piano carried to the office above. Perhaps she could play for him now and he would enjoy it, even if he never came seeking it out. Her world was filled with so many "perhaps" lately.

Taking a seat on the wooden bench, Mara flexed her fingers, letting the inspiration take root. As the first three notes came to her, she envisioned Gannon standing at the center of the maze. She thought of his rough, masculine hands and how delicately they caressed the vibrant four-season roses. There was such reverence in his eyes, such grief.

Mara once thought him filled with nothing but bitterness. Now she saw he felt so deeply. She understood that. To feel every emotion burrowing into your heart could be painful. Better to wear the mask of manners than let anyone see how greatly the world affected her. Gannon had his own mask, and she didn't blame him for clutching it to his face.

Music poured out of her as her mind wandered where she knew she shouldn't let it. Black eyes appeared in her memory, flashing with an unnatural green. And there was that half smile, confident with a touch of mischief. She let her feelings mingle with the music, each note reflecting her uncertainty, her fear, and finally rising to a crescendo the way her growing boldness had. On the other side, her fingers slowed, taking that blooming, beautiful spark in her heart and making it into sound.

The final cadence held such a painful combination of love and despair that it provoked tears. Mara let them fall unhindered as fingertips glided off the ivory edges and dropped into her lap. They ran down her cheeks and dropped from her jaw onto her clasped hands. She rubbed the moisture between her thumb and pointer finger of one hand, still feeling the echoes of the music in her bones.

"That was breathtaking." Mara leaped so high she bumped the piano with her knee, making it jolt with sound.

"I—" she quickly rubbed the tears away, knowing it would do little to disguise her emotion. "I didn't know you were listening." Though she had hoped he was.

Gannon leaned into the doorframe. "I always come to listen when you play."

"You do?"

"In all my years, I have never heard a musician as talented as you."

Her blush was hot on her skin. "I was made to practice a lot."

"Anyone can practice an instrument. What you do is something more. Your music is visceral."

"Your compliment is most kind."

"Don't do that." He pushed off the door, stepping up to the piano and resting his hand on it.

Mara stared at the keys. "Don't do what?"

"Turn into that princess puppet when you feel uncomfortable. I hate it."

For some reason, that made her want to cry more. *Silly*, she told herself. Gannon clearly hated plenty. "I'm sorry, sire."

He poked her nose with a big finger. "You're doing it again. I want the real Mara, not prim princess Mara."

She was so taken aback by his words that her chin jerked up. There it was again, that green. It was milder this time, muted, but the contrast of green and black was unmistakable.

"Why are you crying?"

She chose her words carefully. "I'm suddenly allowed to want, and it feels...heavy."

"The weight of desire is difficult to bear." He didn't break her gaze when he asked, "What do you want?"

It was the same question she'd asked him yesterday, and she hesitated much the same as him. *You*, her heart begged her to say. But Mara kept the admission to herself, instead answering cryptically. "What my heart wants."

For a heartbeat his expression faltered, disappointment dulling the green in his irises. Then it was gone, replaced with his usual stern look. "Freedom. Choice. Of course."

Feeling uncomfortable, Mara brought up the first topic she could think of. "Have you received word from Calos yet?"

"No," he told her curtly, turning on his heel. Clearly, the moment was over.

"Do you think it will come soon?" She was losing hope that it would come at all.

Gannon's shoulders rose to his ears, body stiff. "No."

His certainty surprised her. "Why?"

He inhaled deeply, then on an exhale said, "Because I never sent my inquiry."

Mara froze in place. Even her heart seemed to crystalize with ice. Never sent it? All this time she'd been hopeful and patiently waiting for a letter that never left this house? She didn't know Gannon well, not nearly as well as she liked to pretend, but the feeling of betrayal that struck her was intense. Painful, even.

It was matched only by her indignation.

Voice shaking, she asked, "Why?" Gannon didn't answer. Mara pushed back from the piano and slammed the cover over the keys. "Why, Gannon? Why lie to me? Why keep me here?" Still, he was silent. "Are you going to return me to my father? Was that always your plan?" Then why entertain her as a guest for weeks? Why not get it over with and take whatever prize he earned from obeying the law?

When he finally spoke, it was in that low, gravelly tone. "I won't return you."

"Then why have you been lying to me?" She cursed the break in her voice, the tears that threatened to fall again. "I trusted you."

Gannon pressed the back of his head to the wall and closed his eyes, exhaling slowly. Mara waited and waited until she realized he wasn't going to give her what she wanted. In more ways than one.

Fine, she wouldn't give him any of her honesty either. Mara stomped past him, racing down the hall and up a flight of stairs. She paid no mind to where she was going, following the twists of winding staircases and the turns of longer and longer halls. Eventually she became aware of how dark her surroundings were, most windows covered with heavy drapes. There was little dust and no signs of decay, as she expected in the west wing of the house, but there was no life either.

This part of the house reminded her of her original assessment of the manse. Each dark, empty room and echoing hall was in mourning. A home cast aside, left grieving for the voices that once filled it, the warm bodies that flitted about during their daily activities.

Mara couldn't recall the specifics of her journey and was sure she would be lost in here for a century. At least then she wouldn't have to face Gannon. She couldn't understand his actions or his dishonesty. What did he plan to do with her?

Her whirring thoughts abruptly quieted when she stepped into a room that was unlike the others. Dim autumn light pooled lazily on the floral rug, illuminating the four-poster bed and the painting above it. A dragon peered at her from over his wings, his back to her. Those green, green eyes seemed alive, the dragon almost breathing. One of Edgar's paintings. It had to be.

She followed the source of light further into the room and found it was only a fraction of what the windows could allow. Pulling back the curtains, she coughed out a gasping breath, dust and surprise robbing her lungs of their air.

Windows stretched from the floor to the ceiling, revealing a picturesque view of the foothills. Fog crept down from the mountain peaks, hiding the jagged rock face and leaving only the fading autumn trees.

Twin doors led to a massive balcony. She opened them, stepping into the whipping winds and immediately shivering. The view was undeniably admirable, but why such a large balcony? Surely it could be enjoyed without stepping a hundred feet away from the house. And what could have caused such damage to the stone? Beneath her feet, Mara noted deep scratches. Almost as if—

As if a dragon had landed here. More than once.

"This is where I used to come to clear my head too." Mara thought she might topple over the railing when Gannon appeared behind her in stealthy silence for a second time.

"Why don't you come here anymore? Why is this part of the house abandoned?"

"Because it reminds me too much of the man I was ten years ago." His forearms landed on the banister beside her, leaning toward the mountains like he might take flight and touch them. "I shouldn't have lied to you."

"I don't understand why you did."

The silence was too long, loaded with emotion he refused to show. "I—I was being selfish."

Mara followed the shifting of a low-hanging cloud with her gaze. "Selfish how?" Her heart squeezed, afraid of what he might say. Hopeful for what he might say.

Gannon turned on her, gaze a gleaming green, voice a match for the mountainside. "I didn't want you to leave."

She tilted her face to meet his, gravitating toward him the way the clouds clung to stony outcroppings. "Why?"

"You are a very unique woman. I don't know that anyone else has been gifted the opportunity to see you under all those courtly manners."

"None but you."

His hand was jarringly warm as it cupped her face. "I find I'm becoming addicted to the privilege of seeing you." Gannon was reminiscent of the mountains above them, rugged and unyielding. Imposing and tall. Harsh, but so very beautiful. A force of nature. "It's dangerous for you to look at me like that, Mara."

"I promise I won't hurt you."

His chuckle was a vibration, one she felt more than heard. "Shouldn't I be the one to make that promise?"

"I'm not as fragile as you."

"Then I won't have to worry about doing this." He kissed her. Maybe he wasn't a mountain at all, because surely mountains could not be so tender.

Mara had never been kissed before and had no idea what to expect. She knew some people considered the action romantic, but she hadn't figured out what was special about it. Now she understood. A mouth was used to speak, and not always with words. Gannon's lips told her secrets he'd been harboring for weeks, secrets that matched her own. The kiss started with sweetness, but quickly became incendiary with want.

Gannon was hot, a fire encased in human flesh, and the contact with him was beginning to make Mara ignite.

She felt starved when he pulled away, as if she'd taken only one bite of a five-course meal. His forehead came to hers, and he closed those strange eyes, breathing heavily. It was a plea when he murmured her name, but she wasn't sure what he was begging her for. More? Less? Was his mind wandering to all the ways it was wrong to be with her?

His eyes snapped open on an inhale, breathing out a growl. Then they were kissing, moving, stumbling from the balcony as the wind urged them on. Mara lost her breath when the bed came up behind her and she fell onto it. Gannon pounced, pressing his body atop hers. Every bit of him was hard and muscled. If he wanted to, he could take her right now, and she couldn't stop him.

She *wouldn't* stop him.

Mara knew this was indeed as dangerous as he claimed. There was no regaining her virtue once she'd lost it. What they were doing should be exclusive to a marriage bed. But this was part of having the freedom to choose. She chose him, even if she could never have him the way she wanted. Even if her father's rule kept her from keeping him as her own.

"Please, Gannon."

His body writhed over hers, the thick weight at the center of his hips pressing between her legs and making her insides feel volcanic. "Please? Please, what?"

"I want—I want to give myself to you."

"I want to take you." He growled, hands pushing up her skirts. With a yank, he ripped her frilly undergarments away, smoothing his palms over her thighs, slowly moving higher.

A throb that matched her pulse pounded in her core. She needed him to touch her there. Mara had never felt so desperate for anything in her life. But he was toying with her, trailing hands up and down her legs, licking at her mouth, grinding his hips against her.

"That's all I get? One little please?"

"Please, Gannon. I want you." Her back arching off the bed toward him, she murmured, "I love you."

As if the doors to the balcony were thrown open, frigid air blasted around them, freezing Gannon in place. The green vanished from his eyes and he whipped his hands from her. A moment later he was scrambling backward off the bed, jaw locked and brows low.

"Did I do something wrong?" She already knew the answer. Her slip of the tongue was too much. Gannon didn't want her the way she wanted him. He was merely sating his masculine appetite. A princess was a rare treat indeed.

"I won't make this mistake a second time."

"Mistake?" Devastation speared her heart.

"You're not for me. You can't be."

"Gannon—"

"Go, Mara. Leave me." She didn't move from the bed. His snarl was vicious and inhuman when he charged her and shouted, "Leave me while you still can!"

Fueled by shame and heartbreak, Mara obeyed. Somehow, her feet found their way back to the eastern portion of the manse. She didn't stop when she reached familiar ground, running down the stairs, through the kitchen, and toward the stables.

"Mara?" Elsie's voice followed her. "Are you alright?"

No, she wasn't all right. She wasn't all right for most of her life. Now she never would be. *Mistake*. Gannon called her a mistake. And wasn't that the truth?

Mara was blind with emotion as she searched for the stall housing a familiar red mare. In her time on the Black estate, Edgar was kind enough to show her how to saddle a horse. She wasn't strong enough to hoist the saddle up herself, but she could at least put on a bridle, so she had reins to steer the creature this time.

The horse obediently trotted from the barn when Mara kicked her haunches. Clearly the animal wasn't pleased to return to the Black-wood, but her snort was the only protest she gave as they headed for the road. Elsie and Nigel were shouting after her. She ignored them.

Somewhere in the Blackwood was a fork in the road. She hadn't seen it in the dark, but she knew it was there. That fork led to many places outside of Dunhill, Calos being one of them. She didn't have proper supplies to pass through the mountains, and an early winter storm was all it would take to end her.

At least she would die free.

That was all she had anymore.

CHAPTER 12

T HE BLACKWOOD WAS NO easier to navigate in the daylight, its name a fitting descriptor. Even as the canopy thinned and the leaves blanketed the understory, the light struggled to penetrate the trees. It was as if there was an aura of darkness that covered the wood, blocking out the sun and leaving the tree trunks no more than gray shadows. Mara's horse whinnied uneasily and deep in her chest, she made a similar noise.

It was foolhardy to ride off into the Blackwood once. To do it twice was a death wish. Why was she so incapable of thinking before acting?

After what felt like hours, Mara came upon a fork in the road. Only it wasn't marked. Clearly someone used the other road because the plants weren't creeping over it to reclaim the soil, but she couldn't be certain where it would lead. She took it regardless. And the next turn and the next turn until she was hopelessly lost. Though, could one be lost when they didn't know where they were or where they were going?

Hours crept on and eventually her horse tired, both from the ride and the anxiety that had her tense and wary. Mara had little interest in staying a night in the woods, but it appeared she'd left herself no choice. Tomorrow—if she made it that far—she would swallow her pride and find her way back to the Black estate. From there, she would have to decide where she could go. Clearly, Calos wouldn't be an option without an escort, and by the time she found one, the weather wouldn't allow for safe travel.

The Gods must have been smiling upon her for once. They came upon a crystalline brook surrounded by lush, mossy banks. Both she and her horse drank greedily. There were more flying bugs than either of them were happy about, but the water's edge was the only place where viny plants hadn't taken up resistance, thorny and eager to grab unsuspecting passersby.

Mara was surprisingly unafraid as she settled her back against a tree. What danger could they encounter out here that would be worse than a dragon? Not that they were safe from having another meeting with the Beast of the Blackwood. For some reason, she didn't think she would see him again. Not the way she had the first time.

Her mare didn't share in her confidence. The animal spent hours pulling at her bridle, shuffling her feet, and chuffing. Mara thought they might never sleep, instead waiting out the darkness until they could make their way back out.

And it was dark. So very dark that she could no longer make out the silhouette of her horse. Mara wasn't sure if her eyes were open or closed. They must have been closed because she startled awake, alerted by her horse that something was amiss.

Strange glowing orbs hovered in the distance, bringing with them a rumbling noise. The closer they came, the louder her heart pounded. What other mystical creature was wandering these cursed woods?

It was nothing mystical that came her way, she realized as the sound of wagon wheels on rough road became recognizable to her. The orbs that danced and shimmered were torches, lighting the road in an eerie glow. Naïve as she was, Mara didn't think to hide herself or her horse. She didn't think to climb atop the mare and bolt into the night. Why would she, when she had the good fortune of meeting fellow travelers? Perhaps they could point her where she needed to go.

They stopped not far from her, a man dismounting from the wagon

A chill zinged up Mara's spine as three more sets of boots crunched on the road as men climbed down. "What's a pretty lady doing all alone in the Blackwood? Don't you know it's not safe? There's a dragon about."

"I know. I've seen him."

The man chuckled, ripping a torch from the wagon and waving it in her face. "I doubt that. You wouldn't be in such pretty shape if you had."

Mara covered her face, temporarily blinded by the torch. When her eyes adjusted, she recoiled at the man facing her. Broken teeth were framed by a greedy, shallow smile. His crooked nose moved as he murmured, "Gods. You're the missing princess. There are leaflets all over Dunhill with your face on 'em." That smile stretched, making his beady eyes scrunch up. "They think you've been stolen. You don't look stolen to me. Boys! Come get a gander at what we've found."

"A woman?" Another voice asked.

"A royal reward for all our hard work."

Mara backed up, but it was too late. An arm caught her from behind and lifted her off her feet. Her horse screamed as she did. The sound was utterly useless. There was no one out here to hear them.

❖

GANNON

The sun was setting by the time Gannon garnered enough control of himself to leave the Baron's suite in the west wing. That was also how long it took for the taste of Mara to fade from his lips and the scent of her arousal to dissipate. He was well aware that he was a bastard—a cruel bastard that deserved none of the moments she'd given him during her time here.

To keep her here because he couldn't let her go was selfish. To keep her here and reject her when she admitted love for him was a grade so far beyond selfish that even the Gods didn't have a word for it. But how could she love him? When she wasn't his mate. Lady Fate had not ordained their meeting.

Or had she? Because even now, his dragon's vehemence was flooring. And he wasn't alone in his affection for Mara. Gannon was fond of her. The laughter she let out, as if it was a secret she knew she shouldn't be sharing, filled his heart with a unique sense of joy. Thinking of it as he stood alone on the frigid balcony overlooking the mountains, he realized he couldn't remember Madeline's laugh. Didn't it also bring him joy? Shouldn't he remember vividly if she was the woman meant to be his eternity?

Gods damn him. Could he really have been wrong?

Yes, answered the dragon furiously. *You rejected your mate. You sent her away.*

If Gannon didn't share a body with his dragon, the beast would be ripping his limbs off right now. For ten years, he wallowed in self-pity and heartbreak because of a rejection—a rightful rejection given the circumstances—from the woman he thought to be his mate. He nearly lost his mind over it.

And now he'd done the same to Mara? To innocent, precious Mara. She'd done nothing for him but offer kindness. Was it possible for her to forgive him for his cruelty?

If she was his, she would have to. Wouldn't she? Damn him! Why was it so hard for him to be certain?

Elsie must have been reading his mind, because she shouted, "You're an idiot!" from the bottom of the stairs as he descended.

Nigel and Edgar flanked her, each of them giving him thunderous looks. So, Mara had told them. Of course, she had. They'd become her friends, and they cared for her wellbeing. Even his housekeeper was better to her than he was.

"You can't speak to me that way. I'm a baron."

"I don't care if you're the king of the whole fucking world." Nigel barked. "You ought to be ashamed of yourself."

"If it makes you feel any better, I am." He sighed. "I loathe myself."

"What did you do to her?" Elsie's voice was low, her expression lethal.

"That's between Mara and me. Shouldn't you be cooking dinner for her...or something?" Gannon had no interest in drawing Mara's attention with the commotion and embarrassing her further. He would give her time to lick her wounds and track her down tomorrow.

A muscle ticked on Elsie's face, making the scar over her eye tighten. "We can't serve dinner to someone who isn't here."

"What?" he boomed. "What do you mean not here?"

"She means the princess took her horse and left this afternoon." Nigel crossed his arms, repeating Elsie's question. "What did you do?"

Gannon ignored him, shouting, "Where did she go? How long has she been gone? None of you went after her?"

"Edgar did. He lost her." Elsie told him.

"*Where?*"

"The Blackwood."

Gannon was out the main door and stripping from his clothes before the last half of the word was breathed. Mara alone in the Black-wood. She was *lucky* it was him that found her last time. The dragon kept the other predators away—both animal and man. But the dragon had scarcely been to the woods in weeks, too distracted by Mara's presence to leave the estate.

"Will you admit it now?" Elsie hissed.

"I don't have time to argue with you," he growled back, his voice already breaking up as the transformation began.

"She's the one!" she shouted after him as he took to the sky, stretching his wings and scenting the air. "You wouldn't be going after her if she wasn't the one."

Truth. It was a truth Gannon felt in his bones. Now, knowing she meant to leave him, knowing she could be in danger or worse, he knew beyond doubt. *Mate.* Mara was his mate. He'd been so wrapped up in his past heartbreak that the half of himself that was man refused to acknowledge it. But the truth was always there.

Madeline was a pretty face with a coercive tongue. When they met, he was newly a baron and suffering from the loss of his father. She was the perfect balm for his wounds. And she'd been so eager for his attention.

As he searched the forest from the sky, following the faintest hints of Mara's scent, he replayed his interactions with Madeline through clearer eyes. She was always coy with his brothers, inciting jealousy and making him earn her affection. When they visited the estate, she was rude to Elsie and the others. More than once she threw fits when Gannon didn't bring her expensive enough gifts.

And there was her most egregious act. When he admitted what he was to her, she betrayed him. A mate would never—*could* never do such a thing. Gannon had been so fixated on finding a mate that he created one out of the wrong woman, and it nearly cost him his true mate.

But it wouldn't. Gods, he had to pray it wouldn't.

Night fell, and his eyes shifted, adjusting to the darkness. Above the trees, the stars and moon lit the way, taking him west. She must have thought to make it to Calos. Her scent thickened over a darker part of the forest, but when he caught it, a vicious growl rose in his throat. It was tainted with a pungent note of fear.

Men's voices carried through the trees as he descended, much too thrilled for Gannon's liking. "Come back here, princess!"

"That bitch broke my nose!"

"You'll get a chance to pay her back, Malik. Got'cha!"

Fabric ripped, and Mara screamed. The noise was nothing compared to the roar he released as he landed atop the wagon parked in the middle of the road. Wood crunched beneath his weight. The horses driving the wagon screeched and bolted, dragging broken remnants behind them. Poor creatures would likely get stuck and devoured. Gannon couldn't care about horses just then.

"Gods! It's *the Beast*!" The man closest to him stumbled backward, pointing. What a boring choice for last words.

The next man stood between Mara's attacker and Gannon; a blade grasped in his fist. He swung the thing with a broad arch. It scraped across the scales of Gannon's neck. It would have been a killing blow were he a weak and frightened fawn. He dispatched this man as well.

Two men remained. Both sprinted away from the scene. The one atop Mara tripped over her torso, kicking her in the ribs as he fell forward. Gannon paid him back in kind, stepping on his back until his spine cracked. He would have left the man to suffer, but his groans of pain were loud, and he didn't want to disturb Mara more than she already was. When he was finished, he gave the body a shove with his foot, sending it far away from her.

Hoofbeats boomed through the trees as the last man made his escape. Somehow, he'd managed to untie Mara's horse and climb onto the animal. Both were terrified by him. Gannon desperately wanted to give chase, but Mara was huddled on the ground, clutching the remnants of her dress to her chest. There wasn't a chance in hell he would leave her like that.

Her tremulous body seemed so small among the trees. Suddenly too aware of the gore painting his face, Gannon rubbed his snout along the nearest trunk. It wouldn't eliminate the evidence of his violence, but hopefully it would make him less intimidating.

Mara's chest heaved with panting breaths as he approached, though he wasn't sure it was due to his presence. Her eyes were locked on her torn gown, lost in a vision of horror as she processed what had nearly been done to her. The rage that left bloody limbs lying on the road was alive inside of him, roiling lava that hadn't caused nearly enough death. Or perhaps it meant to burn him from the inside out, punishing him for his own role in this terrible event.

Trying to calm himself, Gannon lowered to his belly, face pointed in Mara's direction. He wanted to shift and hold her in his arms, but he was wary of causing more shock.

Those sweet brown eyes turned sharply in his direction. "You came for me."

He stretched his neck as far as it would reach, placing his nose within reach of her hand. *Of course, I did.*

Hands still shaking, Mara carefully rested her palm over his snout. "I knew it was you."

How could she possibly know?

"Your eyes are unmistakable." He chuffed, rubbing his face against her. "Please take me home."

Gannon obliged, carefully lifting her with his front two feet and cradling her to his chest. She wrapped her arms tightly around his, and when he was comfortable that she was secure, he pushed off with his hind legs and took to the sky.

The journey home was quick. He made sure of it. Gannon shifted fluidly the moment his feet touched down in the garden, taking Mara in his arms and carrying her to the house. Elsie was waiting for them in the foyer, wringing her hands, face pale.

"Thank the Gods! Mara, are you alright?" She crowded around Mara, who insistently climbed from his grasp and burrowed into Elsie's outstretched arms. He supposed he deserved that.

"Oh, Elsie, I was so foolish."

"Don't worry, love." Elsie soothed Mara's back. "You're home now. We'll get you all cleaned up." Even as she murmured comforting words, Elsie glared lethally at him. "Come along. I'll draw you a bath and get you some new clothes." Gannon moved to follow, but she clucked her tongue and shook her head vehemently.

"Elsie—"

"Give her some time," she whispered over her shoulder, quietly enough that only he would hear. "Trust me."

Gannon tried but ultimately failed to do as Elsie asked. He paced anxiously outside Mara's door, occasionally pausing to listen for any sound beyond the swishing of water. More than an hour passed before Elsie slipped from the chamber, ripped dress bundled in her arms.

"She doesn't want company."

"I need to see her."

"She doesn't want to be seen."

"You can't keep me from her." He growled, dangerously close to snapping. It was only guilt that kept him at bay for so long. What happened was his fault, and he knew it.

"I can't." Elsie agreed. "But I can tell you from experience, humiliation does not fade faster with an audience."

With that, she was gone, leaving Gannon to battle silently with himself. Eventually, whatever decency he possessed was lost, and he found himself knocking on the door, calling, "Mara?"

The sight he was greeted with when he stepped inside nearly shattered him. Mara was crouched on the floor, almost hidden by the bed as she leaned against it. Her knees were curled to her chest, arms hugging them tightly. Gannon was such a bitter, broken man that he might have broken his mate too.

Gods, he prayed as he hovered in the doorway. *Please let her be okay.*

CHAPTER 13

MARA

GANNON WAS STARING AT her. She could feel the weight of his gaze and hated that it comforted her. There were so many confusing thoughts trying to seat themselves in the forefront of her mind, and she just wanted to silence them for a time. Gannon was a dragon—*the dragon*. The fabled *Beast of the Blackwood* that haunted the nightmares of children. How was it possible?

Did the logistics of it truly matter? He was a dragon, and he saved her, but only after sending her away and breaking her heart. Mara had established many times over that she was a foolish, naïve girl and had no business claiming she was in love with anyone. What did she know of love? What did she know of the world? So little that strangers came upon her and meant to—Gods, what they meant to do to her—and she was helpless.

Mara quietly said, "I wish to lie down."

"I'll stay with you." He stood in the doorway, a hulking shape that devoured every free inch of space.

"I will politely decline, sire. I'm afraid I'm in no shape for company."

"No shape for company?" His voice raised and quickly lowered again when she flinched. "Don't speak to me like I'm some courtier."

"Forgive me."

"What happened to you? Where's the real Mara?"

You happened to me! She wanted to scream, shame and humiliation writhing in her stomach like an angry serpent. *Those men happened to me!* **You** *happened to me!*

"Please leave me be." Her voice was quickly losing that practiced crispness. She needed him to leave. Mara's entire body shook, her bones creaking with the violence of it, and she was going to fall apart whether he closed that door.

"Mara—"

"Please!" Tears burned her cheeks, and the plea was little more than a croak. "Please let me be."

"I can't." He took a step forward and then hesitated, backpedaling to post up in the doorway once again.

Mara turned away from him, covering her eyes with her hands as if she could press the tears back in. "I wish to be left alone."

"I'll be here. Just outside." His voice came from the hall.

Part of her wanted to rush over and slam it in his face. The other part was relieved he was staying. That poor, pitiful part of herself that believed he might still want her the way she wanted him, even after what happened. Her tears fell harder as she mentally wounded herself, whipping her mind with insults the way her stepmother would whip her flesh to punish her for all of her atrocious behavior.

When her eyes were finally dry, Mara unfurled and stretched her legs. They always hurt as bad as her back after a punishment because she would spend the night curled on the floor just as she did tonight. It comforted her when she was a small, frightened girl, and it comforted her now too.

"Gannon?"

He was crouched before her so fast that she gasped. "I'm here."

Mara tried not to lean into his hand on her arm. She didn't want to lose herself in her want for him again and wind up mortified with an aching heart. "I think you need to explain yourself to me."

Sensing her hesitation, he moved back, settling on the floor in front of her and resting his elbows on his knees. It was jarringly casual to have a baron sitting on her chamber floor. Then again, she was a princess with damp hair, huddled in her nightgown, weeping under the bed.

Gannon heaved a sigh. "Where do I begin?"

The wry note in her tone surprised her. "With the dragon."

That odd purring noise filled the room. "He likes the admiration in your voice when you talk about him."

"He can hear me?" Her eyes rounded. "Is he...inside you? Does he shrink?"

Gannon chuckled. "It's hard to explain. He is a soul, and I am a soul. We each get a turn ruling the physical realm."

"So, he's...like the voice in your head?"

"That's an excellent way of putting it. Though, most people don't have a conscience that threatens to burn things and bite limbs off."

Mara paled. "Do you enjoy the violence?"

He scratched at the layer of stubble on his jaw. "Not always."

"Do you hurt innocents?"

"I try not to. Lately my dragon he, ugh...he's gone a bit wild. You have to understand, dragons are very territorial, and a lot of unsavory folk try to pass through the Blackwood. Sometimes the dragon can't tell the difference between a traveler and a poacher or smuggler."

"And you—he—likes to hurt them?"

"Most of the time, he's indifferent. He considers it a chore. But tonight—" A growl cut the air, and emerald gleamed menacingly in his eyes. They were undeniably dragon in that moment. "Tonight, he enjoyed it."

Mara considered, tilting her head to study the man before her—if he could ever be considered a man. It should bother her. Even if he did rescue her, the violence and death should sit wrong on her conscience. Somehow, it didn't. She couldn't muster any sympathy for those men. What they tried to do to her—how many women had come before her? How many times had *they* harmed innocents?

"Those men, were they smugglers?"

"Yes."

"What do they smuggle?"

"Anything. Weapons, stolen art, fabric, exotic animals. The worst of them smuggle people. Often women and children kidnapped form poor villages on the outskirts of kingdoms. They bring them through the Blackwood and south of Calos, to the cape of Castrel. From there, they put them on ships to Gazar." The tightness in Gannon's jaw told her precisely how he felt about those evil men and their malicious business.

"Gazari still keep slaves? Even after all of these centuries?"

"It is the reason the Gazari king has such inflated wealth. He makes his gold off the backs of others. My people are not safe from his imprisonment either."

"Your people?" She leaned forward, uncoiling a bit more. "So, you consider yourself something...*other*? Not a man? Not like me?"

"I am a man, and I am more. My kind are known as *Drakonmein*. We have existed in this world for as long as ordinary men have. Some say the Gods created us. Others believe we all descend from one father, a hero who committed such great acts that the Gods gifted him a dragon to live in his chest and defend his people." Gannon mirrored her movement, sidling closer. "We used to live openly, but greedy men became jealous of our power and fearful of our wrath. Some grew to hate us for our propensity for, er, stealing."

"Are you a thief? Is that where your wealth comes from?"

"No, my grandfather earned his wealth as most men do. Dragons *do* enjoy treasure, but not always in a literal sense. We treasure things of beauty...creatures of beauty."

"Like swans?"

His booming laughter smoothed some of the jagged edges of her splintered heart. "Not quite."

Mara couldn't help smiling just a little. "Why does that amuse you?"

"Have you ever heard of dragon brides?"

She had, and recently too. Queen Sophia of Calos was the first in a century, offered by her father to the dragon that threatened their flocks and farmers.

Long ago, it was a custom for each kingdom to sacrifice maidens to appease the dragons that ruled the realms. They were stronger and more powerful than even kings, thus royal families were not exempt from offering one of their daughters as offerings. In her history lessons, Mara learned that Dunhill was one of the kingdoms that stopped the dragon bride tradition.

It was her great-grandfather's doing. He cherished his only daughter more than his crown and feared she would be chosen by the dragon, devoured as a sacrifice or spirited off to bear dragonlings in some mountain cave. When he decreed that not a single maiden was to be brought to the hillside where sacrifices were made each decade, there were tragic repercussions.

"You—you steal maidens?" She scuttled away, her back hitting the mattress. "Is that why you've dismissed all your staff? So that they won't see you kidnapping women? *Devouring them?*"

"Of course not!" He put placatory hands up. "Don't be frightened, Mara. It's nothing like the tales. There is a terrible misinterpretation of *Drakonmein* and their proclivities by common man. Our history and traditions have been forgotten." Gannon stilled, hunching his shoulders as if it would make him less imposing. It didn't. "A dragon, like an ordinary man, takes only one bride. The difference is that we have little choice in the matter. Upon our arrival into this world, Lady Fate divines a bride for us, a woman whose soul is chosen to match our own."

"And you kidnap her?"

"Ugh, sometimes. Some dragons do, yes. The drive to find a mate is unrivaled by any other instinct. We have very, very long lifespans, and oftentimes the women meant for us have not yet come into this world when we have. The wait for them can be excruciating. Imagine knowing there will be a perfect mate for you but waiting centuries for her. When you *do* find her, you may become a bit...overzealous."

"*Centuries?*" Mara interrupted. "You've lived *centuries?*"

"No, but I could have if I hadn't found my mate."

Disappointment settled in her gut, heavy as a stone. "So, you have found her? Your bride?" That was why he dismissed her as a mistake. She wasn't his bride, and it would be a heinous act of infidelity to be with her.

Gannon sighed heavily and leaned back onto his elbows, reclining with his head slanted toward the ceiling. "I thought I found her ten years ago, but that woman was very wrong for me. She betrayed me, and as a result, I killed her father."

Mara sucked in a breath. Just how many people had he killed?

"I met her just after my parents died. I was newly a baron and grieving deeply. All I wanted was to find my mate, to seek comfort in that bond I knew existed for me. Madeline was a shopkeeper in a wealthy city southeast of here." The name sounded poisonous on his tongue, and she was surprisingly relieved. If he'd sounded heartbroken over this woman, it would only make her jealousy and disappointment worse. "Her father was a con man who disguised himself as a traveling merchant. I think she took one look at me and saw the opportunity for wealth and power she and her father always wanted.

"I took one look at her and thought she was mine. She was a beautiful woman, or so I thought. Now, she appears a snake in my mind. I can't fathom how I ever convinced myself she was the one."

"Desperation makes men foolish," Mara murmured.

"Indeed." He hesitated then, a haunted, hollow look dulling his dark eyes. "I almost—" He cleared his throat. "I almost bonded to her."

Her throat was suddenly dusty as well. "Bonded?"

"Dragons don't merely take a woman as a bride. When they become one in flesh with their mate, they also become one in soul. We share a bond with our mate that links our lives together. If she were to die, so too would I pass away. The love between dragon and mate is that fierce."

"Beautiful." She whispered, forgetting he would hear.

Gannon smiled sadly. "Beautiful and tragic. I don't know what would have happened had I given it to the wrong woman." His finger traced a pattern on his knee, softening the image of him even more. Vulnerability clearly made him uncomfortable. "When I confided in her what I was, she was frightened. She didn't admire the dragon. She thought him a monster—*me* a monster. Madeline fled the estate and didn't return for two weeks.

"I gave her time, knowing that my mate could not bear to part with me anymore than I could bear to part with her. Upon her return, she brought her father. There were demands for a dowry. He already had plans drawn up for a wedding. He even expected me to invite your father to the event. I can't clearly recall what happened after that." His gaze grew bleary. "There was a disagreement. Words were thrown from all parties. Then Madeline's father threatened to tell the world what I was, to bring hell on my family and draw every eager young knight from every kingdom to slay the Beast of the Blackwood and his kin. He knew not only my secret but my brother's, and he was going to expose all of them."

Mara scooted forward, gripping his hand tightly. "You killed him to protect them."

"I hadn't planned to, but my dragon, he was enraged. It took all the control I had to keep him from going after Madeline next. He always—*always*—thought her a wolf in sheep's clothing, but I ignored him. I was so very blind, and it nearly cost me my sanity. I've spent the last ten years slowly going mad, losing the battle with my dragon." Gannon tightened his fingers around hers. "He wanted only one thing, and he was going wild in his hunt to find her."

"Who is she?" Mara asked, trying to be kind. Surely it wasn't Elsie? There was heat between her and the baron, but it wasn't the kind lovers shared. More like the combined loyalty and derision siblings had for each other.

"You don't know?" His smile was brilliant, the first unrestrained and honest smile he'd given her. "It's you, Mara. *You.*"

"Me?" She released his hand, regaining the space between them by standing. "But you sent me away."

"I shouldn't have. I'm really, very sorry that I did."

"I don't understand." Suddenly the room felt too small, and her head was swimming. "You've avoided me, refused to dine with me. You lied to me, then you *kissed me*, only to chase me from your home."

"I didn't intend for you to leave my home. I only needed to gain some distance from you—to clear my mind."

"Why?" she demanded. "You cannot say that I am some—some woman *destined for you*. Not after the way that you've behaved."

"I can!"

Mara paced to the fireplace, tossing her hands up. "*Why?*"

"Because I was afraid." He spoke so softly she scarcely heard him. "I was beginning to see what you were to me, and it frightened me. I got it wrong once, so very wrong. I feared what might happen to you if I was wrong again."

She gave him her back. "And how are you to know if you're wrong again?"

"I know that I'm not."

"Such confidence after all that ambivalence."

"I was walking the world blind. A fool with my eyes closed and my ears tuned away from the blaring sound of my heart and the beast who shares it with me." The heat of his body engulfed her from behind, but he didn't touch her, only whispered against her neck, "I am a coward and I shied away from your beauty. You left me breathless from the start, and I feared you would smother me."

"I would never smother you. Freedom is the greatest gift you can give the one you love."

He pushed away, settling in a chair some distance from her. "Is that what you want, Mara? That I set you free?" She didn't respond. "Say the word and I will bring you to Calos as soon as the sun rises."

That new life she longed for was dangling in front of her; she need only grasp it and finally, *finally*, own herself. Live for herself. She could pursue her passions—write music and spend afternoons tending to lovely, blooming things.

But she'd done that here, hadn't she? Each day she spent in the Black estate, she felt a little more unfettered. Her heart came alive, her music flowing into her fingertips so readily. The constant fear of reprisal over every perceived failure was dissipating, replaced by a boldness she hadn't known she possessed.

That new life she longed for had already started, and it was rooted here. With Gannon and Elsie, Nigel and Edgar. Could she...could she stay here? Could she safely hide away from her father and make a home for herself? *With Gannon?*

"If I were to say no, what is the alternative?"

"I would beg you to stay with me." He pressed his palms together as if in prayer. "I would offer you all of my wealth, my home, my heart, my *soul*, if only you would stay with me. Give me a chance to earn your love. I yearn for it. I have yearned for it for much of my life."

Mara closed her eyes, remembering the weightless feeling of flying. "I have yearned for you too."

"My beautiful, beautiful Mara." He rose, standing before her and taking her hand in his. "You deserve much more than I have given you." He kissed her knuckles. "You are a rare and precious gem, and I should have been treasuring you."

A blush pushed away some of her chill, but she fought against it. Ignoring the fluttering creatures in her belly, she removed her hand from his and stood tall. "I have been rash in everything I've done since I left my father's home. I can't be rash in this and risk my heart."

It wasn't a rejection like the one he'd thrown at her, calling her a mistake, but it hit him just as hard. "What are you saying, Mara? Will you not give me a chance to be good to you?"

"You have been good to me, and I am grateful." She smoothed the fabric of her nightgown, finding comfort in her ability to fidget without repercussion. "But—"

"Don't say it." Gannon cut her off. "Whatever it is, don't say it." He rubbed his jaw. "Let me court you. I'll do it right. Let me court you and then make your decision."

Mara suppressed her smile. It was hard to imagine Gannon as the courting type. His manners weren't refined enough for that. "You want to court me?"

In truth, she hadn't planned to reject him, only to tell him she needed time to find her footing. Time to learn who she was without the confines of her strict family rules. But wasn't this the perfect solution? Gannon would be forced to behave properly, and they would both resist the temptation that overtook them the day before. To have joined with him the way she intended would have been…a mistake. He was right in that. Passion unchecked was as dangerous as a wildfire.

If he was going to light her up, she wanted it to be a slow-building heat.

"Yes." He was almost pleading. "Anything to keep you here. To give me a chance to take back the time I squandered."

"Time you squandered feeling sorry for yourself."

Gannon's eyes became black slits. "You're starting to sound like Elsie."

"Elsie is a brave woman. I should like to learn some of her courage."

"You are more courageous than you think."

They stared at each other, and Mara felt that dangerous wildfire heat licking at the back of her neck. Another loaded moment and it would engulf her.

"I'm tired," she blurted, crossing her arms and moving toward the bed. "It's been a dreadfully long night."

"Of course. You should get some rest. Do you need anything?"

"No, thank you, Gannon."

He smiled at the use of his name. "I'll be right here if you need me."

Her steps faltered. "Right where?"

"Here." He dropped back into the chair by the fireplace.

"Don't you think that's inappropriate?" she challenged.

"No." His face was to the fireplace, but she could see the smirk in his profile.

"It's improper for a suitor to be present in my private chambers."

"I imagine it's improper for me to see you in that lacey nightgown too. Have you noticed how sheer the bodice is?"

Mara gasped, instinctively covering her breasts. "You are a lewd man!"

"And you said you *yearn* for me, lecherous man that I am."

"Ill mannered, patronizing lout. Shoo!" She stomped back over to his chair and flicked her hands at him as if he were a pest in her garden.

The dragon shone green in his eyes. "There she is."

"I have been here this entire time. You should not be. Don't you have a bed waiting for you?"

"I haven't used it in weeks."

"Where do you sleep then? Do you roost like a bird?"

"A bird? Do I look like I have feathers?"

She shrugged. "You have wings."

"I do not *roost* like a *bird*. When I sleep, I sleep as a man." His nose wrinkled up in distaste at the comparison.

"Then go wherever it is that you sleep as a man and do that, please. I thank you for your hospitality, *sire.*" Hands still covering her breasts, she marched back to the bed and thumped into it, scowling. The gall of that man! He'd only just apologized for chasing her away, only just rescued her from violent ruffians, and now he was forcing his way into her bedchamber? She had to hold back another smile. This was precisely how she imagined a courtship with him would go.

"Very well," Gannon said curtly, rising from the chair and striding to the doorway. He stopped when he got there, putting his back to the frame and sliding down the floor. Head leaned at a painful angle, he closed his eyes and feigned sleep.

"What are you doing?"

"What you've asked me to do. This is where I sleep."

"You're teasing me."

His lips curved. "I am not. I have slept here for thirty-eight nights."

Mara did the math in her head. "You've been sleeping in my door-way every night since..."

"Since you arrived, yes. I may be an idiot, but my dragon is not. He insisted I keep you safe while you sleep, and so I did." That was...thoughtful. Strange—very strange—but thoughtful.

Ignoring him, she flopped her head onto the pillow and pulled the blanket up to her chin. The room felt chilly again, even with the roaring fire Elsie had started. Mara rolled to her side, then back. She flipped over onto her stomach, shifting her legs four different ways and finding none of those positions comfortable. Finally, after what felt like hours, she turned onto her back and murmured, "Gannon?"

"Yes, Mara?"

"If you insist on staying, then you may as well sleep comfortably."

He sounded a little too eager when he asked, "Are you inviting me into your bed?"

"Gods, no! You haven't courted me for five minutes yet."

"It's been more than five minutes."

"Sleep on the chaise lounge or stay on that floor. I don't care." She huffed, rolling back onto her stomach and squeezing her eyes shut.

Floorboards creaked, that familiar sound that comforted her each night she lay sleepless in an unfamiliar bed. It had been him. The presence that called her mind into rest was him. She realized then that she believed everything he claimed about fate. There was more to what she felt than the simple infatuation of a maiden given a choice of partner for the first time. Mara fell for him so easily, her heart growing love for him even as he was brusque and absent.

"You're a terrible liar."

"And you're a terrible sleeper." She retorted drowsily. "Goodnight, Gannon."

"Dream of me, Mara."

She couldn't help her giggle. The Gannon she was seeing now was so unlike the cold baron she'd met in his sitting room the first night she was here. Mara had admired that version of him, even as he frightened her, but she liked this version much better. He made her feel weightless.

He made her feel uncaged.

CHAPTER 14

GANNON

THE SHEETS WHISPERED BENEATH Gannon as he slid carefully across the mattress. Soon enough the sun would rise, and Mara would rise with it. After the night she had, she needed rest. But she was always early to wake, and he suspected today wouldn't be any different.

Her eyelids fluttered as a dream walked beneath them, plush lips pinched slightly. The temptation to run his thumb over them was nearly impossible to ignore, but he managed. Silky black curls fanned across her pillow. They were a match in coloring and complexion. Blacks were always fair of skin and black of hair. His mother had been as blonde as a mountain peak, yet each of her sons favored their father.

Gannon caught his hand as he realized it was wandering toward those luscious curls. She would be cross with him if she woke to find him here, no doubt. Or perhaps she wouldn't. Mara was a funny creature, all grace and manners at first glance. Underneath the frills of that stupid etiquette was a soft heart, a woman who laughed easily, a creative soul whose music flowed as wildly and unplanned as the plants creeping out from the Blackwood to overtake the surrounding fields.

Someone tried to break her—her family, the ones who should have been cherishing her—and they failed. Mara had fine cracks along her frame, sensitive places that he'd seen and been wary of touching, but she wouldn't shatter like porcelain. Beneath those cracks was a solid, unshakeable foundation. Gannon had every intention of adding to it, building her up until she never cowered before anyone again.

And Gods help her father if he ever got his hands on that rotten king. A man was meant to treasure his daughters, not train them the way he trained his caged beasts.

Never mind him. Gannon would show Mara what it meant to be treasured. He would earn her forgiveness for his horrible, idiotic behavior, and he would woo her so thoroughly she would never want to leave his arms. Or his bed.

Blood rushed from his overactive brain to the lower part of himself that was equally overactive lately. Now he'd gone from pushing a boundary to thoroughly crossing it. Lying beside her to watch her sleep was innocent enough. Lying beside her and fantasizing about the way her cunt would grow slick for him if he took one of those beautiful pink nipples in his mouth was vulgar. Deliciously vulgar.

They were such beautiful nipples, peaked and straining against her nightgown. Was all women's sleepwear so revealing? Perhaps he should have barged into her bed chambers sooner.

Suddenly he was alert, fluid and graceful as he left the bed and hurried to the window. He cracked the glass pane, careful not to allow the frigid morning air to worm its way in and disturb Mara.

Horses. He wasn't mistaken. Gannon heard horses approaching the estate. From here it was impossible to tell what direction they were coming from, only that there were few of them.

Damn. Damn, damn, damn. He knew the king would come calling eventually. It wouldn't be hard to hide Mara from him for now, but what about in a year? What about when he took her for a bride? Would she be content to live in an unkempt house with few staff and fewer amenities? That would likely be the only way to keep her safely tucked away. Otherwise, gossip would spread, and the court would grow curious about his mysterious bride and request an audience.

A simple baron, no matter how wealthy, could turn down a request for an audience from the king only so many times.

Gannon took the stairs two at a time, skipping the last few with a leap that had his boots pounding into the floors. Elsie appeared in the doorway of the dining hall just as he landed, her bronze face uncharacteristically pale.

"Is it the king's messengers?" She asked breathlessly, clutching the rag in her hands without mercy. He wasn't the only one who'd grown attached to Mara.

"I don't know."

"Shall I bring her to the west wing?"

"No, let her rest. It's not as if they'll ask to search the house."

"I should hope not. We have more than one secret in this decrepit place." Ah, there was the usual Elsie. She continued muttering to herself about "dragons" and "arrogant men" as she ascended the first flight of stairs. She only made it to the landing before she froze, eyes widening when the front door flung open.

A cold gust of air burst into the foyer, carrying stray autumn debris and depositing it on the otherwise clean floors. Three mud-coated pairs of boots thumped one after another over the threshold, not bothering to stop and clean themselves before stepping onto the antique rug that decorated the front hall.

"Eoin," Elsie whispered, the longing in her voice obvious.

Eoin froze, his black eyes snapping to the sunset orange of his dragon as his pupils dilated. Every muscle in his body stiffened, his jaw so tight it could shatter. Then, as quickly as they changed, his eyes were back to normal, focusing intently on Gannon.

Elsie composed herself too, storming back down the stairs, rag waving angrily as she chided, "Have you lot forgotten your manners or are soldiers too pea-brained to have any? Off with those boots, all of you! I break my back shaking out this damn rug, and you have the gall to drag muck into my foyer?"

"*Your* foyer?" Amos raised his brow.

"May as well be mine, since I'm the only person in this house who gives two shits about whether it crumbles to the ground."

Eoin dodged her as she came at them with her lethal rag. He tapped Gannon's shoulder and said, "I'll meet you in your study. It's good to see you, brother."

Gannon nodded, watching his retreat without missing the furtive glance he cast at Elsie over his shoulder. That was a puzzle he would never solve.

Clearly, Elsie wasn't the one meant for Eoin, or he would never be able to stay away from her as he did. That didn't stop Elsie from longing for him. The three remaining Black brothers were wise enough not to mention it as Eoin disappeared upstairs.

"Oh Elsie, you beautiful monster, you are a sight for sore eyes." Davin grabbed her around the waist and lifted her into a crushing hug, spinning her before setting her back on her feet. "How I've missed your snits."

Elsie laughed, squeezing Davin. "You brute! Look at you! You must have gained a hundred pounds since you were last home."

He grinned, flexing his arms and showing off his notable muscle. "You like what you see?"

She rolled her eyes, moving on to Amos. Their hug was amiable but gentler, her lips pecking his cheek as she gave him a sisterly caress. "And look at you, handsome as ever. I'm surprised you found the time to train, what with all those books we've been sending you."

"You forget, Elsie dear, I can read in the dark." Amos patted the top of her head.

"Well, Elsie, where's breakfast? I'm starved," Davin boomed, filling the first floor with noise.

"The sun has scarcely risen. If you want breakfast before dawn, you can make it yourself." She gave his arm a playful smack on her way back to the kitchen.

All activity suddenly halted, both Elsie and his brothers turning their gazes to the stairs. Gannon followed their curiosity, pivoting on his heel and finding Mara on the landing above them. Eoin stood behind her, his expression suspicious. Mara was dressed and had obviously left her chambers on her own accord. That was all that kept him from charging up the stairs and throttling his brother. Eoin's body language was too threatening for Gannon's taste.

"You didn't tell us you had company, Gannon."

"I didn't realize it was your business if I had company," he growled back.

"After what happened with Madeline, it's always our business." Eoin crossed his muscled arms, looking every bit the imposing soldier that he was. "And after that letter you sent? You have some explaining to do." He loomed over Mara, asking, "What's your name, girl?"

To her credit, Mara didn't cower beneath his mountain of a brother, though her voice was shaking when she answered, "Mara."

"Strange coincidence, brother." Eoin stepped down the stairs, closing the space between him and Gannon. "Just before we left camp, we received word that the king was calling soldiers down from the mountain to aid in the search for a stolen princess. What was her name again?" He tapped his chin.

"Mara. It was definitely Mara," Davin said, his grin impish.

"Have you lost your Gods damned mind?" Eoin snarled. "You stole a princess?"

"You may be in charge of your soldiers, Eoin, but you would do well to remember who the head of this household is." Gannon bared his teeth. "I don't take kindly to your tone."

"I don't take kindly to you calling us home, only to find out you've kidnapped the king's daughter!"

Mara cleared her throat, tapping her fingers nervously along the banister. "He didn't kidnap me." She paused, glancing up as she considered. "Well, I suppose you did when you snatched me from the Blackwood. He only kidnapped me the smallest bit. And I didn't try to stop him! Does it even count then?" Gannon had never seen her look so flustered. She was beautiful with a delicate blush. He couldn't help but smile, overcome with pride that she was *his*.

Amos' tone took on a note of reverence as he said, "She's yours."

"Careful, brother. Don't forget the last time we didn't properly guard our family secrets," Eoin warned. "Does she know?"

"That you're dragons?" asked Mara.

"I imagine she knows everything now," said Elsie, kicking a clot of mud from the rug with the toe of her shoe on her way out.

Davin chimed in next. "I knew that hat shop twit wasn't your mate. She would have married a gargoyle if his cock was thick and his coin purse thicker." If Mara thought *Gannon* was rude, she was in for a shock. Davin gave their mother heart palpitations with his antics. "On second thought, she couldn't have been that concerned with cock size if she wanted yours, Gannon. Have you found that bastard yet? You sure you're the first-born son and not my homely sister?"

Amos scratched his chin thoughtfully. "You do pout like a girl."

"If moodiness is the defining mark of a woman, then you're all cock-less wenches and I'm the man of the house!" Elsie called from the dining hall, her words punctuated with the clanking of plates.

"Come on, Elsie. No one's moods rival yours," Davin protested.

"She only has one mood." Eoin spoke up in a rare interaction with Elsie. Most visits he scarcely acknowledged her other than to thank her for meals and ask after the house. "Vicious."

Elsie came around the corner, a handful of silverware in her fist. Her caramel eyes narrowed, and she pointed her forks threateningly. "And you best remember that, Eoin Black."

"I wish he would just bed her already. The sexual tension is killing me," Davin mock whispered, rubbing the back of his neck.

"Watch your mouth, soldier. You're in the presence of a princess," Eoin barked in his captain's voice.

"That's what bothered you? Not all the talk about cocks?"

"Davin!" Gannon and Eoin shouted at once.

Gannon beckoned Mara down the stairs, taking her hand and drawing her close to his side. Having his brothers surrounding her as they were was making him edgy.

"You seem almost civilized in comparison," Mara said loudly enough for them all to hear.

Gannon laughed. "Why do you think I'm Baron Black and they're mere ruffians?"

"You're only baron because you had the misfortune of being the first seed father spilled into our dearest mother. Don't get a big head. Prick." Davin waved the insult his way, striding toward the dining room.

Eoin leaped forward and caught Davin's arm. "You're forgetting something."

"No, I don't think I am."

"Boots. Off."

"You're not my captain here. I'll wear boots wherever I please." He shrugged off Eoin's hold.

"If you leave a mess for her, I'll skin you."

"Her? Her who?" Davin cupped his ear, walking backward into the dining room with his signature grin.

"If you love her so much," Amos grunted as he kicked off his boots. "Why don't you marry her?"

Eoin's face shuttered so rapidly he could have been turned to stone. His eyes glazed, and his fingers twitched. Gannon had a sudden instinct to get Mara away from his brother. Very far away. The beast inside Eoin felt wrong, monstrous and angry. Disturbingly angry. Smoke scent filled the air, and pressure made Gannon grit his teeth to keep his own dragon at bay. Gripping Mara's elbow, he quickly led her into the dining room.

"Let me formally introduce you to my brothers. Now that you've seen how utterly uncouth they are."

"I expected nothing less. I've seen your paintings, after all." She smiled over her shoulder at him, not an ounce of timidity after being ambushed by his boisterous family.

The front door slammed behind them, and Gannon released the breath he'd been holding. Perhaps he wasn't the only Black brother whose dragon was causing him trouble. Amos and Davin met his gaze, their expressions serious as they both acknowledged what he was saying without words. The four of them were long overdue for a meeting.

"You showed her the gallery?" Davin groaned. "Why do you insist on keeping those dreadful paintings?"

"I thought they were rather charming." She let Gannon pull out a seat for her, sitting poised and prim at the head of the table.

"She also finds Nigel charming, so don't take it as a compliment," Elsie commented.

"My favorite is the one with the mermaid."

Amos groaned a second time. "It was meant to be a self-portrait."

Of course, Davin found a way to make a joke about Amos having flippers. The dining room was filled with laughter and raucous voices. Eoin rejoined the chaos at some point, smiling when appropriate. His eyes still looked a bit too vacant for Gannon's liking.

Things got rowdier when Mara requested Nigel, Edgar, and Elsie join them at the main table. "I don't see why they shouldn't. They work hard to maintain the house all on their own. They're more family than staff."

"You are a very unusual princess." Amos remarked. "Are you sure you're the daughter of Dunhill?"

Mara's smile faltered. "Quite."

"Not anymore." Nigel chuckled as he sauntered in with a tray of bacon, his belly bouncing beneath it. "She's the lady of the house now."

"Am I? What will you do if I go off to Calos after all?"

"Steal you back," Gannon growled.

She eyed him, trying to judge if he was serious. He was. Deadly. "I thought you said you didn't do that."

"Well, I have, apparently. Only a little, so I'm not sure it counts." Her napkin rose to cover her laughter, as it usually did. He stilled her hand with his. "You are free to laugh here."

"I am," she whispered. "I am free here."

The confidence with which she stated it filled him once more with that sense of pride. In appearance, Mara was delicate and feminine. In character, her strength could rival even Eoin's.

Gannon became aware of the sudden silence in the dining room. He glanced up to find not only his brothers, but Elsie, Nigel, and Edgar watching him with astonishment written plainly on their faces.

"What are you all staring at?" he snipped.

"We haven't seen you act so much yourself since father died," Amos told him.

Davin raised his mug of tea. "It's good to have you back, brother."

"Seems this was a wasted trip." Eoin grumbled into his forkful of eggs. "Unless we're here to retrieve the princess, but she doesn't look stolen."

"We aren't bringing her home." Davin whined before Gannon had a chance to voice his protest. "Look at her. She suits us."

"Us?" Amos quirked a brow. "She's not a family pet, Davin."

"She could be." He shrugged innocently. "If Eoin keeps his trap shut."

Elsie's accusatory question sliced through the argument that ensued. "Why is it a wasted trip if you get a chance to visit your family? It's been nearly a year since you've come home."

Eoin refused to look at her when he explained, "We aren't sitting by the fire and playing drinking games up there. We're training for war. Tensions are high. They say the king needs only strengthen his forces before he's ready to break the treaty."

"All the more reason to visit while you can."

On one side of the table, where Elsie scowled over her plate, the air became so chilled that ice crystals could have formed on the dinnerware. On the other hand, heat roared from his brother so violently that Gannon could almost hear the crackle of flames. There was always banter between Elsie and Eoin, and their teasing sometimes escalated to sniping, but this was different. Elsie's picking at him was meant to provoke, churning up some aggressive ire that Eoin was not very successfully containing.

Years ago, Gannon had assumed Elsie was Eoin's mate. Why else did he hover over her so obsessively? Their relationship had changed sometime in the last few years, and clearly Gannon had missed it. How long had they been at each other's throats with him listlessly ignoring the warnings put off by Eoin's dragon? Such a waste the last decade had been. Gannon hadn't only failed himself. He'd failed his brothers, his friends, and he nearly failed Mara. All because he couldn't remove his head from his ass.

"Thank you for a lovely meal, Elsie. Would you mind accompanying Mara to the garden while my brothers and I meet in the study?" The chair beneath him was forced back with the momentum as he rose. Gannon tried to remain as calm as possible, though the dragon in him was trying to peel his skin back and maim his brother. Eoin was not safe to be in this house with Gannon's mate unless he could get a hold on that monstrosity inside of him.

Mara glanced at his half-finished plate, perplexed. "Will I see you when you've finished fulfilling your daily duties?"

He took her hand and kissed the top, taking his time to feel the softness of her palms. "Sooner. I won't be able to keep myself from you long enough to finish my tasks."

She blushed, casting their audience a furtive eye. To think only weeks ago, he planned for this day to be one of his last. His brothers were meant to be here to end him. Instead, they would be witnesses to his new beginning. Gannon wasn't losing his mind at all. He was only mad in the way a *drakonmein* became in the presence of an unclaimed mate.

He was so distracted by the vivid fantasies that came alive as he thought of claiming her that he almost forgot his brother's fury. The four of them stomped up the stairs, filing into the baron's study. The space was much too small with four hulking men taking residence in each corner, and it only felt smaller as Eoin sucked in a harsh breath, clearly battling the beast within.

"It seems we need to talk." Gannon sat behind the desk, pressing his fingertips together.

"Indeed." Eoin turned half-yellowed eyes on him. "You have a lot of explaining to do."

"As do you, brother. As do you."

CHAPTER 15

MARA

"Forgive me if I'm overstepping," Mara began, huddling into her cloak as the breeze became a strong gust that hinted more of winter than autumn. "But how did you become Gannon's housekeeper? You seem to know the Black brothers very well."

Elsie squeezed her arm. "I love it when you overstep, Mara. If a question isn't uncomfortable and too personal, is it even worth asking?" She smiled, but the lively gleam was missing from it. "I was barely a woman when Eoin brought me here. He was newly a soldier, returning home from training to mourn the loss of his parents, when he found me on the road outside my village."

She stared over the treetops. "My father was killed..." Her steps faltered, and she shook her head, trying to drop the weight of her memories with it. "My father was killed, and I had nowhere to go. Eoin was kind enough to give me sanctuary at the Black Estate."

So, Mara wasn't the first wayward young maiden who ended up on the doorstep of the Black estate.

"Gannon offered me an education, the opportunity to find service with some lord's wife. Even the thought of it made me snore." They skirted the edge of the maze, turning toward the front gates where the apple trees were shedding the last fruits of the season. "The late Baron Black senior and his wife had only passed away weeks before my arrival. The household was in disarray, the brothers lost without the guidance of their father. I needed a way to keep my hands busy, and Gannon needed someone to help him run the estate as he adjusted to his new position as baron. It all happened very naturally."

"And you stayed, with no staff to help you maintain such a grand home?"

"The Black brothers are my family." Elsie had a stricken look about her, an uncharacteristic sadness that was so deep it must have burrowed into her bones. "I'll tend to this house until I'm a wizened old lady."

Mara chewed her lip. Elsie said no question was interesting unless it was too personal, but it felt so wrong to ask her to divulge the history of a relationship that clearly pained her. Curiosity was always one of her strongest traits, yet Mara became excellent at repressing it. A princess was never to question and never to pry.

Mara didn't want to be a princess any longer.

"Are you in love with Eoin?" She blurted rudely.

Elsie's chuckle held a touch of her usual warmth. "Is it that obvious?" Mara nodded. "He was the first man to ever treat me kindly. We were good friends once, thick as thieves. I wrote to him each and every week while he was in training. When he went to war..." She clutched her throat, paling. "I wrote to him then too. I knew he wouldn't receive my letters until—unless—he returned to camp, but I wrote him anyway. It's impossible not to love someone when they share all of your secrets."

Don't ask. But she couldn't help herself. "What happened? You don't appear to be so friendly with each other any longer."

"I don't know," she answered honestly. "Perhaps it's simply because I am not the one for him and he feels entertaining my attention is a betrayal to *her,* whoever she may be."

Mara took her friend's ungloved hand, warming it with the wool that blanketed her own fingers. She recalled the way her heart felt as if it was crumbling into pieces when Gannon sent her away and tried to imagine enduring that ache for a decade. Lady Fate was a fickle player, and her games were the source of most conflict. Silently, Mara prayed that Elsie would find happiness, the joy of being adored, even if it was not with Eoin.

Elsie was a spirited and brave woman, but there were ghosts that hovered darkly around her soul. They made brief appearances in those coffee-colored eyes, haunting vestiges of the rough life that came before her time at the Black estate. Perhaps someday Mara would ask about that, too. Today, Elsie bared enough of herself. No use rubbing her raw with talk of old memories.

Mara knew her life was luxurious and simple compared to a woman like Elsie, but she wasn't unfamiliar with ghosts. There were one or two pestering her on her darker days too.

"And what of you, sweetest Mara? You've been fawning over that big oaf for weeks. I selfishly want you to fall in love with him, so you stay here and keep me company. There are too many men in that house." She wrapped her fingers more tightly around Mara's. "We wayward women need to stick together."

Shoulders back, chin out, Mara put on her very best princess voice, informing, "The Baron Black has begun courting me."

Elsie snorted. "Courting you? Why on earth would he do that?"

"I would like him to."

"You want to be courted? By *Gannon*? The man doesn't know which of the forks he's meant to use for salad, much less how to court a noble-born lady."

Mara couldn't help her smirk. "I know."

Another snort. "I have underestimated you, princess. This is going to be an amusing show indeed."

They paused in their teasing, Elsie going completely rigid as a sudden noise carried over the wind. The gates to the estate were open—as they always were. Who would make it through the Blackwood and intrude unannounced when there was a dragon about? In answer to that question, six riders trotted up to the gate, bearing a bright red flag with the king of Dunhill's sigil.

"Go inside, Mara. Right now. Go around the maze and enter through the kitchen," Elsie commanded. "*Now, Mara.*"

Mara obeyed, her steps as quick as she could make them without drawing attention. If a cloaked woman took off running from the king's messengers, they would grow understandably suspicious. She was breathless by the time she reached the kitchen door, pushing it closed behind her and leaning against it. The tie of her cloak was too tight, and her trembling fingers struggled to undo the knot. Exertion had her body breaking out in sweat, the cloak suddenly feeling suffocating.

"What's the matter? Where's Elsie?" Nigel rushed from where he stoked the cooking fire, bushy brows covering his eyes.

"She's at the gate. The king—" She choked on her words, stuttering, "Royal messengers have just arrived."

"Let me help ya." He made quick work of her cloak, hanging it on a hook beside his apron. "Those stairs'll take ye up to the southern hall on the third floor. Take it to the end, turn right, and go up the next flight of stairs. Don't come out of the west wing until we retrieve you, ya hear?"

Mara nodded her head so wildly that her vision blurred. Hands fisting her skirt, she hurried up the stairs, following Nigel's instructions until she found herself in a familiar room. The doors to the balcony were still open in the Baron's chambers, and a scattering of leaves had made their way in. She shut both doors, fighting against the wind, and busied herself starting a fire. All the heat from her escape was gone, leaving the chilly air to pick at each droplet of sweat and cause her shivering to worsen.

Hours seemed to pass as Mara waited, pacing the room, training her ears to pick up even the slightest hint of voices. If Gannon was playing a good host—which she hoped he was—then the messengers would have been invited into the sitting room on the eastern side of the house, as far from her as they could get. Even a dragon wouldn't have skill enough hearing to catch their conversation from here. The only noise Mara heard was a skittering that sounded awfully rodent-like.

Eventually she ended up perched on the bed, knees tucked to her chest to keep a rodent from nibbling her toes while she was distracted. Her weeks at the Black Estate felt like a dream, not always pleasant but thrilling, nonetheless. Now she'd woken from her slumber with a startling jolt, returning to reality with the pins and needles of sleep still tingling in her limbs. She wanted nothing more than to stay in this home, laughing with her new and unusual friends by her side, smiling secretly at Gannon.

There was a beautiful future in the gleam of those black and green eyes. But that too was a dream, a fantasy that was perhaps too frivolous for the life they were both born into.

Mara picked at the hem of her bodice, reveling in what may be one of her last chances to fidget. She was a naïve, foolish girl, wasn't she? No matter where she ran or who she tried to become, she would never be free.

CHAPTER 16

GANNON

GANNON KNEW THE EXPRESSION he wore was grim as he entered the baron's chamber. Mara was reclining on the four-poster bed. For some reason, he knew that was where he would find her, returning to the place they'd nearly become one.

"Is it bad news, then?" She looked much the same as the night before, curled into herself, eyes downcast.

"It's worse than I expected. Your father is an opportunist, it would seem." It wasn't only news from the king's messengers that had him fighting the need to spread his wings, either.

The conversation with his brothers might have ended dangerously if they hadn't been interrupted by a panicked Elsie. That distracted Eoin thoroughly enough to halt his thundering rage. When had the man become so angry?

"I have every right to be angry, Gannon!" Eoin had shouted at the accusatory question. "You called us home to *kill you*. For years, our reassurance that Madeline was not your mate has fallen on deaf ears. You have been absent even when you are right beside us and now, we come home to suffer the guilt of ending your life because you've convinced yourself you've gone mad, only to find you prancing like a lovesick puppy after a missing princess!"

"I didn't expect to find my mate weeks before you arrived," he countered.

"Where did you find her exactly?" Amos cut some of the tension with his curiosity. "She's presumed kidnapped."

"She escaped."

"Women don't typically need to escape from their own home the night before their wedding," Davin pointed out.

"She didn't want to marry her betrothed."

"Many women don't, but duty binds us all," Eoin snarled. "You can't possibly understand the chaos this has caused."

"Are you suggesting I should have returned my *mate* to be married to another man?" Gannon stood from behind the desk. "The King of Dunhill is a monster! Do you have any idea how he treats her? A woman shouldn't *cower* over spilled tea. I would have helped her even if she weren't my mate. Her family has gravely mistreated her, and she does not deserve to face their wrath again." He pointed at his brother. "Enough about Mara. The real concern is you, Eoin. What's wrong with your dragon?"

Eoin's eyes became a startling shade of sunset. "This is what war looks like on our kind, brother. My dragon is none of your concern."

"It's my concern when you can scarcely control yourself long enough to eat breakfast. How long have you been struggling?"

"I'm not struggling. Unlike you, I can control myself just fine."

Gannon looked to Amos and Davin to aid his argument. "You are a different man from the one that left this house ten years ago."

"*Ten years* ago. Do you have any idea what's happened in those ten years? Were you so lost in your own grief that you didn't realize there was a war on the doorstep of Dunhill? I became what I had to and there is no changing that. Leave it alone, Gannon."

"Perhaps Gannon has a point," Amos chimed in. "You haven't shifted with us in so long I can't remember what your dragon looks like."

"I prefer to shift alone."

"You didn't use to," Davin pointed out.

Eoin snarled in their direction. "Stop pretending to be concerned with me! I am as I have been for many years. What are you going to do about the princess? What if someone discovers she's here? They'll have your head, Gannon! Do you realize that? They'll have your head, and then she'll return to where she came from with no one to keep her safe from this family that supposedly torments her."

"I'm already building a plan. I'll have paperwork forged for her, identifying her as a foreigner. There is an easy solution to Mara's problems, I simply haven't found it yet. You're trying to distract us from what is clearly an issue with *you*, Eoin." Gannon planted his hands on the desk. "Is this about Elsie?"

The voice that spoke was not Eoin's, but something much darker—something lethal. Like stones grinding together, the voice of his dragon uttered, "Do not presume to speak of her." Just as the tension was escalating to a dangerous boiling point, Eoin went rigid. His orange eyes shot to the door, and he rushed to it, flinging it open and bellowing, "Elsie?"

Elsie appeared in the hallway, breathless and befuddled by Eoin's sudden looming presence. "I need to speak to Gannon."

"Are you alright?"

"It's urgent, Eoin." She glowered at him, pushing him out of the way and entering the office. "There are king's messengers in your sitting room."

He'd known they would come eventually, but their timing was terrible. Gannon should have spent the weeks that Mara was with him coming up with a plan, not battling between his instincts and his guilt.

"Please bring them refreshments and let them know I'll be with them shortly." Gannon straightened, blinking rapidly to clear his head and ensure there wouldn't be a hint of his other half showing in his eyes when he stepped downstairs. "This isn't over, Eoin. I'm worried about you, brother."

Gannon wasn't sure, but he thought he'd heard Eoin mutter, "Years too late," as he left the study.

"Who is he blaming for taking me? Calos? Gersia? Brula? Perhaps he'll claim a Gazari warlord snatched me and declare war on the islands." Mara pinched her thumbnail between her teeth. "I'm so foolish. I should have known he would seize upon my disappearance. It's very likely that my father knows I am a wayward bride."

"According to his messengers, he believes Queen Sophia of Calos used her dragon as a distraction to have hired swords snatch you. He is taking it as an act of war and plans to declare as much to them come winter's end. There is an execution order out for whoever is responsible for kidnapping you." Gannon sank onto the edge of the mattress, rubbing his face.

"An execution order?" Her heart began pounding loudly enough for him to hear clearly. "Gannon, I have to go back."

He whipped around, snarling, "You will not go back." She flinched, a hint of that frightened girl returning. "I'm sorry, Mara. I didn't mean to frighten you. Today has been tedious, and I'm..." Gannon wasn't accustomed to explaining himself and found it more difficult than he expected. Especially because if he was truly honest with her, he was afraid.

Afraid of what might happen if someone discovered her before he could find a forger, afraid for his brothers if there was a war. It was obvious that war had been hell on Eoin, and he was the strongest of them in character. Would Davin lose that mischievous sparkle in his eyes after years of bloodshed? Would Amos still find joy in book collections and riddles if he was haunted by the faces of soldiers that he killed?

"Worried." She finished for him, sliding to a seat at the edge of the bed beside him and taking his hand. "You're justly concerned."

"Yes. A bit."

Her sigh carried the weight of the world. "This is my fault. I should never have left. I should have fulfilled my duty, as a good princess is expected to."

Gannon twisted, cupping her face and sternly saying, "This was coming regardless. Your father would have found another opportunity to break the treaty."

"He is a warmonger," Mara agreed. "He has been incensed from the moment he signed that treaty."

"The terms were to no one's liking."

"If he had his way, I do believe he would like to be king of Svalta. He will never be satisfied with the power he has." She wrapped her fingers around his wrists, gently rubbing some of the tension away with her thumbs. "We can't win a war against Calos. Even if he could get his troops safely through the mountains, they are no match for a dragon."

"Indeed." He snorted. "Burne is a monster. I wouldn't bet in my favor if I faced him."

Burne's father came to visit the Black estate less frequently as his son grew older. Gannon's father, too, had reservations about letting the boys play unsupervised once they'd begun making their first shifts. Young dragons rarely felt territorial in the beginning, but they were prone to bouts of aggression that could be rather violent. Amos had his first shift during Burne's last visit, and the results were not pretty.

None had expected the demon that ripped from his brother's skin. Of the four brothers, Amos was the steadiest in his studies. He was kind of heart and strong in his faith. The dragon gifted to him by the Gods was very much the opposite.

Burne was as gentle with the youngest black brother as he could be when they fought, but the golden dragon that lived inside of him was double their size and didn't take kindly to unprovoked attacks. If not for Burne's father, Amos could have died that day. That memory felt as if it had been in another lifetime. So many years passed without word from his childhood friend that Gannon wasn't certain Burne still lived. Now, news of him was bittersweet as he realized his brothers might be on the opposing side of a war with Burne.

"I've written a letter to Calos. Edgar is sending a courier to the mountain outpost as we speak."

"Ah, now you'll write a letter to Calos." Mara tried for humor, but the joke fell flat, lacking the amusement necessary to make either of them smile.

They held position on the edge of the bed for a silent stretch, each lost in their own thoughts. When Gannon forced himself out of his head, eyes seeking to trace the outline of Mara's beautiful face, he found her brow furrowed in deep concentration. Her mind whirred so rapidly that he could almost hear it.

Suddenly she blurted, "How do you give a mate a bond?"

Heat roared to life in his veins. "What?"

"When you talked about this bond, you made it sound like a gift you would give. Do you want to give it to me?"

"Gods, Mara, you should be careful how you speak about such things." The beast between his legs came alive, *very* eager to give it to her. "The bond is a connection of souls. Two souls become one when two flesh become one."

She blushed as deeply as a rose petal. "Oh." Lips pressed together, she asked, "So you nearly gave me your bond the other night when we were in here?"

"Yes," he growled. "My dragon desperately wanted to be bound to you."

"And you? Do you want that too?"

"Yes, Mara. Yes. I want nothing more than for you to be mine for the rest of my days." He stood, shifting his legs in an attempt to readjust the significant weight pressing on the front of his trousers. "But you must understand, a bond is more than a marriage. I would be irrevocably tied to you. There is no going back from a bond. It binds our lifetimes together. If you were to die, so too would I. Your every joy and pain would echo through that bond into me."

"If I am sad, would you know?"

"Indeed."

"So, you will also feel it when I'm happy." She smiled at him, shy and sweet and very enticing. "What of me? Will I know your joy too?"

"Yes, and if you were mine, you would feel my joy each and every day for as long as we live."

"I want to feel your joy, Gannon."

"I was going to marry you first. Court you the way that you desired." He paced before the bed, fighting the urge to pounce on her and do exactly as she asked and then some.

"I've changed my mind. I don't want to wait." Mara stood, her blush still flaring on her cheeks, and stilled him with a hand on his chest. "Tonight, I wish to be bound to you."

Gannon fisted his hands, jaw tight. He'd nearly done this ten years ago. He'd nearly done it again last night, with a woman so different from Madeline they were scarcely of the same species. Some minuscule part of him still feared he was seeing only what he wanted to see in

Mara and that the bond he would create between them would be warped and wrong.

But when he inhaled the sweet floral scent of her, there was no wrongness in his lungs. When he stepped closer, cupping the nape of her neck and pressing her to his chest, the warmth of her did not feel out of place against him. Finally, he kissed her, tasting those delicious lips and purring at the pleasure pulsing all the way to his cock from that simple act.

Mine. The beast inside of Gannon held himself in predatory stillness, watching to see what would unfold, waiting for the perfect moment to strike. He'd been hunting Mara from the moment he scented her, stalking the prey he intended to catch and keep. *Mine.*

The word became a chant in his head, repeating louder and louder until it drowned out all coherence. Gannon made a terrible mistake ten years ago that almost ruined his life. This was his redemption, the cleansing love that would wash away his past. Mara opened his eyes when he'd been too blinded by grief and loneliness to see the world around him. Now he intended to repay her by opening his heart and giving her all that he had to give—his soul.

"I will cherish you for as long as we live." Gannon's lips followed the curve of her jaw. "I will give you everything that your heart desires. Your happiness is my greatest wish."

"I desire only you," she murmured.

He couldn't fathom why, but he wasn't interested in finding the answer now. That desire she spoke of was evident in the way her hands delicately climbed his chest to brush his cheek. It was a delicious perfume in the air as he continued kissing down her throat, inciting her arousal.

"My treasure," Gannon murmured, his tongue darting out to taste her neck. His voice deepened, and he knew if he were to look up, Mara would see the dragon in his eyes. "I have been waiting to devour you for a long time."

She gasped when he lifted her, carrying her the short distance to the bed and laying her on her back. The urge to take her *now*, to bind her to him and make her a permanent fixture in his life was so very tempting. But Mara could only give her maidenhead to him once and he wanted her to relish this consummation as much as he would. His hand was following a languid path up her calf, climbing further and further up her gown, when Mara stiffened.

Gannon froze, fearing he'd overstepped. His palm rested on top of her thigh, and he stilled it. That was when he noticed the texture of her silky skin had changed, the smoothness replaced by raised patterns. He'd forgotten the scars that Elsie whispered about the first night Mara was here.

For a moment he had to close his eyes, willing the rage to recede before it poisoned his time with her and sent him soaring over the Blackwood to hunt down her father. What kind of torment left scars on such delicate skin?

Mara shuffled further up on the bed, straightening her gown and avoiding his eyes. "I'm sorry. I've forgotten that I'm not beautiful."

"Nonsense. You are the most beautiful creature that my eyes will ever look upon."

"You haven't seen me," she whispered. "I am damaged."

"Let me see you," he beseeched. "Let me admire every inch of you."

"I will revolt you." She clasped her hands together, and he knew she was retreating behind her mask.

"Don't you dare, Mara. Don't keep yourself from me." Gannon wrenched his shirt over his head, quickly undoing the buttons on his trousers. Mara's pupils became black pools as he dropped the last of his clothes, standing proudly naked before her.

"I am yours. Every flawed inch of me."

She barely breathed, "You are flawless."

"And so are you." He took his hand and wrapped it around the base of his cock, drawing her attention there. "Does it look like I care about scars? I ache for you. Let me see you."

Mara kept her gaze on his length as he slowly stroked himself, her tongue wetting her lips in an absent gesture that told him that he had brought her mind back to where he wanted it. Still fixated on him, she unlaced the side of her gown, letting it slide from her shoulders, over her hips, and past her legs to pool at her feet. The blush returned then, and she squeezed her eyes shut, undoing her undergarments without looking.

His lungs stuttered, and Gannon had to remind himself how to breathe. She was perfection embodied, with thick feminine hips, small, plump breasts, and legs built to wrap around him while he pleasured her. There *were* scars. He planned to memorize all of them. The most prominent was a burn that spilled between both her thighs, as if hot liquid had been poured there. The incident with the toppled teacup returned to him, and he had to drag himself to the present to keep from speculating. Mara would tell him the story if she wanted to.

She turned in a slow circle, arms tense as they resisted covering her. Thin white lines were carved along her back and down to her backside. They appeared to be marks left from lashings. Many of them. Whoever gave them was careful with their hand, lining them up so that none would show above the collar of a modest gown. Someday, Gannon intended to kill whoever did this to her, even if it was the king himself. Tonight, however, he needed to show her how little he cared about her imperfections.

Mara was stunning, more beautiful than any fantasy he could craft with his mind. Prowling with all the grace of the predator he was,

Gannon came up behind her, taking her wrist and spinning her. He guided her fingers around his cock. "I *ache* for you, Mara. You are a goddess, and I am humbled that you would give yourself to me."

Her lips allowed the smallest moan to escape. "Oh, Gannon." She caressed him, her fingertips tracing the plump veins along his length. His cock throbbed madly in her grasp, jumping at her touch. Delicious honey-soaked rosebuds bloomed in the air as she admired his hardness. "You are so unyielding. What if I can't take you into me?"

"You can. I'll make sure of it." And he did, tossing her back onto the bed and pouncing on her.

Gannon started at her neck, sucking soft flesh into his mouth and leaving his mark. After tonight, she would wear a permanent one. He was slow and precise as he moved to her nipples, sure to kiss every space between them and her collarbones. Arching, Mara gripped his hair as he teased pink peaks with his tongue. By the time his fingers traced the wet lips of her core, any shame was forgotten.

And when he finally pressed those fingers into her, mimicking the way his cock would be sheathed in her, she knew nothing but his name and the pleasure he gave her.

"Gannon!" she cried. "Gods, please, Gannon! I need you."

"I'm right here." He purred, licking the inside of her thigh where her wetness had spread.

"I need all of you." She sat up, gripping his forearms and beckoning him forward. "I want you to fill me. I want to be under you. Let me hear you cry out my name in rapture, too."

Driven by her fervor, Gannon leaped onto the bed, spreading her thighs wide and lifting them. With one rough thrust, he penetrated her, burying himself hilt-deep into her burning core. Belatedly, he realized he should have eased into her so she could adjust to the size difference between his cock and his fingers. Her breath was a shallow mewling, and he leaned to kiss her face, murmuring, "I'm sorry, Mara. Is it too much?"

"Not enough." She panted, kicking his hips with her heels. "I want more."

Surprised, he drew back and thrust again. "More than that?"

"Yes. More. Don't hold back." Her hand found the back of his head and gave his hair a demanding little tug. "Lose yourself in me."

Gods be damned, she was going to make him come undone with those words.

That was precisely what she had intended. With every desperate groan of her name and every sharp thrust, Mara's cries became louder. Her thighs rode his waist and her arms tangled around him, always trying to draw him closer. The pleasure only intensified for the both of them as the first hints of the bond came together. Gannon could feel the way she rode the edge of climax, chasing it as his pelvis rocked into that sweet spot at the apex of her core. He knew how she delighted in the hardness of his body against her—inside of her.

Mara was aware of absolutely nothing but him, and that knowledge fed the monstrous ego he shared with his dragon. Grinning at the drunken look on her face, he paused when he was fully sheathed in her. She opened her mouth to protest his stillness when he ground into her, satisfying the pulsing need for contact on that most sensitive place. That was all it took for her to melt beneath him, clawing at his back, lifting her hips to ride out her waves of climax on his cock.

Gannon had never seen anything as divine as Mara in the throes of ecstasy. He wasn't going to be satisfied seeing it only once, either.

But the echoes of her pleasure through their burgeoning bond was his undoing, and he couldn't resist the urge to drive into her, once, twice, three times, then freezing as he marked her with his seed.

"You are magnificent." Mara whispered reverently. "I could forsake the Gods and worship only you."

Gannon chuckled, already growing hard again. "I didn't expect you to be so eager."

"Why wouldn't I be eager for that?"

"Why indeed." He kissed her long and slowly, luxuriating in the buzzing magic that was alive in his heart. "Can you feel me?"

"You're rather large. It would be impossible not to."

"Careful, sweet Mara. You're stroking an already oversized ego." Gannon briefly caught her lower lip with his teeth. "Can you feel me here?" He pressed his palm over her heart.

She mirrored the touch, closing her eyes and breathing softly. Gannon was suddenly overcome with a wave of love and adoration that was not his own. How was it that she loved him? Such a harsh and thoughtless man.

"Yes," she answered quietly. "I feel you."

"Now we are one." He told her. "In the eyes of my kind, we are forever bound." Lifting her arm and turning her slightly, he examined her. There, just below the curve of her shoulder, was a black swirl, like a serpent coiling into itself. "You bear my mark to prove it."

"Your mark?" She sat up, trying to look over her shoulder and seeing nothing. "What mark?"

"Did I forget to mention that part?" Gannon traced the black coil again. "Dragon brides bear the mark of their mate. From what I was taught, each one looks different for every dragon. Yours is black."

Her eyes rounded. "How big is it?"

"Not large."

"I want to see it." Gannon fetched her a hand mirror from the bedside table and helped her turn it just so. "How did it get there?"

He shrugged. "The same way the bond does. Magic."

"Magic." She murmured, a hint of a smile playing on her lips. "Does that make me your wife?"

"No, but you will be soon enough." A sudden hint of despair came through their bond, but as quickly as it came, it vanished, leaving Gannon to wonder if he'd imagined it.

"Soon enough." She agreed. "Until then..."

Gannon didn't need her to complete the thought. With slow, teasing thrusts, he indulged her, making love to her until the hour was late and the moon was high above them.

CHAPTER 17

MARA

MARA'S HEART BROKE A little more with every rise of Gannon's strong shoulders. His breath was a summer breeze against her breasts, and she was relieved she'd asked him to open the balcony doors. His skin always felt warm to her, but the air was sharp with the end of autumn, and she thought perhaps she ran cold. During their love making, she discovered that his kind created heat in excess. She'd been a puddle by the third time and not only because her legs trembled with pleasure.

Gannon made a contented noise, reminding her of a giant cat, as she traced the ridges of his spine with her fingertips. His arms were snug around her, head resting on her chest as he dozed. It wasn't an ideal position to extricate herself from the bed, but she would worry about it soon enough. For now, she wanted to enjoy the feel of him blanketing her while she could.

In sleep, his expression wasn't as stoic. Now that she'd met his family, she saw more of his personality in how he wore his features.

His face wasn't as broad or severe as Eoin—though some of that had to be Eoin's perpetual scowl—nor was his smile as devilish as Davin's. When he was quietly thoughtful, he was missing the intelligent sparkle that made Amos' eyes appear like slabs of shined granite. Of the four brothers, Gannon was the perfect balance between Eoin's brusqueness, Davin's good humor, and Amos' kindness. It was as if each brother chose a piece of Gannon and emulated it. They were similar but they missed the vital parts that made up the whole.

Mara considered herself lucky to have met him. Gannon wasn't the most amiable person, but he was kind when it counted. Smart when he needed to be. Funny when the mood was too tense. It was no wonder she'd fallen so desperately in love with him.

It was because of that love that she had to leave.

She promised herself one night. One night to give herself to him, to make their bond complete. The court would be horrified to know she was no longer a maiden at the hands of a man she hadn't married. But Gannon was right. What they shared was so much stronger than a simple marriage contract. A part of him lived inside of her, thrumming as a constant reminder of the love she bore and the justification for the sacrifice she would make.

Gannon didn't take her father's threats seriously. He was concerned enough, but Mara knew the king of Dunhill too well to take a risk with Gannon's life. Her father loved punishments. Retribution would be had for her disappearance, even if the punished was innocent. Mara should have anticipated this. It was an embarrassment to have your daughter flee from an arranged marriage.

An embarrassment and an opportunity, in her father's eyes. If he had his way, many people would die for the sake of her honor. Or rather, for the sake of stretching his royal reach as far as he could. Father aspired to greatness like no king had ever seen. Foolish of him to think he would win a war against a dragon. But not surprising, either.

It wasn't only for Gannon that she had to return home. Mara would make an appearance; prove to the court she hadn't been stolen by Calos or any kingdom. She would accept her shame and her pun-ishment to save her love, to save his brothers, and to protect the many innocents that stood between her father and his goal.

Gannon stirred as she tried to slip from beneath him. His eyes were dark for a change, a hazy charcoal. The smile he fixed her with was bleary and satisfied. Another arrow pierced her heart. He was truly a work of art. The perfect form, hand shaped by the Gods.

"What's wrong, Mara?"

Mara focused not on her sadness, but her purpose. She pushed the reason for her secret departure, her affection for him, to the place where she felt the bond inside of her. "I'm a bit overwhelmed is all."

"Was it too much? I was terrible at courting you. I should have given you time."

"No, no." She cupped his cheek. "This was beautiful. I'm simply overcome by the way that I love you."

"I have no idea what I have done to earn that love."

"Nor do I." She teased. "You're an ill-mannered brute who listens to no one but himself."

His brows cinched together. "I listen to you."

"Except when I ask you to leave my chamber."

"I did leave. I was in the hallway."

"Ha! That doesn't count."

"Oh, no?" He growled, pressing her onto her back and raising himself over her. Their argument dissolved into a heated kiss, which led to yet another scorching connection.

Mara let the world fade for the time that he was inside her, memorizing the feel of him filling her and the way each muscle moved as he mounted her. She would never forget this night for as long as she lived. It was one of the few times she was truly happy.

The sky was showing the faintest hints of dawn color when Gannon finally fell back asleep. Mara was exhausted but her determination kept her eyes wide and her body restless. It took several minutes to sneak from the bed. He murmured her name, reaching for her in the empty space beside him, and she had to turn away. Looking back would make it too unbearable, so she didn't.

Avoiding Elsie proved to be much more difficult than escaping Gannon. Eoin too was a problem as Mara nearly turned the corner straight into him. His back was to her but there was no use hiding from him.

He sniffed the air loudly and glanced at her over his sizable shoulder. "Where are you off to so early?"

"The garden." The lie came easier than she expected. "Morning air helps to clear my head." She passed him as confidently as she could. On impulse she added a passing comment. "I think Elsie will join me. She wakes before the sun."

Whatever was between Eoin and Elsie, he avoided her diligently. Hopefully he wouldn't follow her if he believed Elsie was with her. And hopefully he wouldn't run into Elsie on the second floor before Mara made it to the stable.

A sense of DeJa'Vu struck her as she walked through the open stable doors, shivering despite her cloak. Venturing into the Blackwood once was impetuous. Twice was madness. A third time made her certain she lacked the necessary instinct for self-preservation. This wasn't a decision made for herself, though. Sacrifice only carried weight when it was done selflessly.

Mara would easily sacrifice herself for Gannon.

Her chosen horse snorted a drowsy greeting, stretching his neck over the stall door in search of his morning food. She'd become quite the equestrian thief lately, hadn't she? Mara was reaching for the latch when a shape slipped from the shadows. Edgar's face was impassive as he stared at her, but his eyes told her that he wasn't without judgment. He gestured with both hands pressed toward his chest, asking, "What are you doing?"

"Would you believe me if I told you I was out for a morning ride?"

He shook his head, lips forming a taut line.

Mara sighed, dropping her hand from the door. "I have to return home, Edgar. If my father finds out I've been here, he'll kill Gannon. Maybe all of you." She smoothed her fingers through the horse's mane. "I can't risk his life. And I can't let anyone go to war over me. It's not right. Without my presence, they can make up whatever lies they please to stoke the fires of conflict."

Edgar considered her, that deep silence of his feeling suffocating as she waited. Finally, he nodded, turning to take a saddle from the rack on the far wall. He worked swiftly to prepare her horse, deftly tightening and adjusting until the saddle was situated as it should be.

Edgar pulled his notebook from the breast pocket of his coat and scribbled fiercely. *Follow the road straight through the gate. Take no turns. It will lead you directly to the castle.*

"Thank you." She whispered tearfully as he handed her the reins. Edgar only shook his head sadly, placing a palm over his heart. Mara understood and she mirrored his gesture. "I shall never forget your kindness. You are the greatest friends. All of you. I am blessed to have known you."

His parting response was a gentle kiss blown from his palm. Mara snatched it from the air, clinging to that imaginary affection until she was well past the gates of the Black estate.

The Blackwood was less frightening now that she'd seen the worst of it. She would be wary of other travelers and listen for the predators known to lurk around trees, but she would not be fearful. None were as ferocious as the Beast of the Blackwood, and she had no fear of him. Already she pined for him, longed for him to swoop down from the sky and bring her home.

There would be no going home. Not until she faced her father.

And two thirds through her journey, Mara began to doubt if Gannon would come for her. Even through the growing distance she felt his panic, then anger. That must have been the moment he realized she was gone. Perhaps she should have left a note and taken the time to explain herself, but she couldn't risk him waking and stopping her. She couldn't risk losing her nerve and choosing to hide from her responsibilities in the Black Estate forever.

The castle gates loomed over her in familiar mockery before she was ready. They appeared ominous in the dulled sunlight of late autumn, a great maw that would swallow her up. At the gatehouse the guards were quick to allow her in, having recognized her from afar. It should have come as no surprise that they escorted her like a prisoner to the throne room, a gloved hand gripping both of her arms.

Her father and stepmother were perched atop their thrones, gilded crowns weighing heavily on their heads. The room was abuzz with the voices of courtiers and servants until Mara appeared in the doorway. A servant standing beside the dais with a pitcher of wine nearly dropped it when he saw her. With a graceful flourish the king rose from his throne, marching to Mara and embracing her.

"Oh, my beautiful daughter, we have feared for you! How is it that you have come to us? Have you escaped your captors? Oh, thank the Gods. Worry not my sweet, our enemies will be punished for this. I have a plan for retribution." His voice boomed through the hall, a performance rather than an actual reunion.

Though her heart pounded, she spoke as clearly and loudly as she could. "I was not stolen father. I left by my own free will. I did not wish to marry so I became a wayward bride."

"Poor girl, you're confused. What have they done to you to cause you to say such nonsense? It was that wretched dragon queen of Calos! Her distraction was meant not for entertainment, but to steal away my most precious treasure. I am not so easily fooled by the likes of her." Father's hand came to the nape of her neck, and he drew her close enough for Mara to smell the wine on his lips as he hissed, "You have shamed me for the last time daughter. When this is through, I will marry you to the most brutish, ugly man that will have you. In the meantime, Lucilla will deal with your wretched behavior as she sees fit."

Panicked, Mara shouted, "I wasn't taken! I ran away! You mustn't go to war over such trivialities." She looked to the courtiers, their faces a mix of shock, horror, and delight at the unfolding drama. "Don't you understand? Soldiers cannot fight dragons! So many will die for naught!"

"The princess is hysterical. Lucilla, please accompany her to her chambers while she waits for the royal physician." The king returned to his throne, waving at the nearest advisor and impatiently saying, "proceed," as if she hadn't barged into the throne room after weeks of absence.

Mara kicked against the guards, yelling louder than she'd ever dared, but it was no use. Door after door was closed behind her, further muffling her noise until she was tossed onto the floor of a familiar room.

"No!" She pleaded on instinct, feeling like a trapped animal as the heavy door locked behind her and her stepmother. There was only one window in the chamber that Mara so often had to call her home and it was covered by a thick black curtain, letting in the cool air, but never the sun. Two sconces with dark colored candles were the sole source of light. Along the walls was a series of hooks that held a thin cane, a switch, and manacles for when Mara was particularly misbehaved.

"Strip." Stepmother demanded coldly. "You have disobeyed every rule that I have taught you, filth."

"No." She shook her head again, fighting the claustrophobia of this room.

"Strip or I shall cut your gown and you will have to march naked back to your chambers when you are done here."

Mara finally obeyed with shaking hands. There was a well of anger inside of her, growing ever deeper with each moment. She wasn't sure how much of it was Gannon and how much was her. She needed to calm herself or risk him taking to the skies and coming here. Mara wanted him safe. That was why she was here. She could endure punishment for his safety.

With detached efficiency, she removed her gown then strode to the slanted wooden table in the center of the room and pressed herself into it face first. She was still as her stepmother attached the manacles to her wrists and her lack of reaction clearly irritated the queen.

"First you will be punished for the shame and humiliation you have caused us. Then for souring a carefully made match. When I am finished, you will tell me where you've been and what you've been doing." Stepmother stayed her hand on the second manacle and with a sharp intake of breath murmured, "Gods have mercy."

A fingertip barely caressed the skin on her left shoulder, where Mara knew she bore Gannon's mark. The delicate black swirl was out of place on her pale skin, the contrast making it obvious in her state of undress. Mara started when her stepmother released a breathy laugh. She glanced back to see the woman clutching her throat, eyes glittering greedily.

"Truly we have been blessed. No greater fortune could befall the king than this." Lucilla grabbed Mara's hair and yanked, wrenching her head back painfully. "A dragon whore, are you? Where is that wretched *Beast of the Blackwood*?"

How could she know what the mark meant? Mara hadn't heard of it until Gannon told her. "I don't know what you're talking about."

"Don't lie to me, girl." Lucilla released her head with a push, smacking Mara's face into the slanted table so hard her nose began to bleed. Then she was gone, slamming the heavy door and leaving Mara half shackled to the table.

Mara considered attempting to escape but there was no removing the manacle without the key. Soon enough her stepmother would return, and the punishment would be more severe if she showed any rebelliousness.

Indeed, the queen did return not half an hour later with the king and the royal physician in tow. The urge to squirm away from them and hide her nakedness grew as they approached, staring at her as if she were one of the exotic creatures father liked to keep in his menagerie.

"It's here, your highness." Stepmother brushed Mara's loose hair aside, curtsying low and moving from her father's side.

"Gods, it's unbelievable." Her father touched the mark on her shoulder with a prodding finger. "Lucilla, you have outdone yourself." To the physician he said, "Do your examination. Quickly."

The physician hurried over, unshackling Mara and turning her onto her back. If he was disturbed by her scars, her nakedness, or the instruments of punishment on the wall, his face did not show it. With a stern expression he pushed her legs apart, lifting a candle high to see her most private place.

On instinct she pressed them back together, crying, "Don't you dare touch me."

"I must for the examination, princess." He explained calmly. "Please hold still."

Mara didn't and in the end, they returned the manacles to her wrists, leaving her helpless as the physician touched her where no man but Gannon should. She refused to shed a single tear, instead focusing on Gannon's roiling rage coming through their bond. Was it directed at her? Would he hate her for what she did, even if it was to keep him safe?

There was no end to her foolishness, it would seem. Did she expect that Gannon would simply let her go? That the courtiers would rally behind her and refuse to support the king in his useless war? *Of course, they wouldn't.* War was profitable for them and so was gaining territory. They cared not for the soldiers who were willing to sacrifice their lives to ensure their families had food in their bellies. Men like the Black brothers were nothing to them.

When the physician was done, he stood and turned to the king. "She is a maiden no more."

"You terrible girl. I raised you so finely and this is how you repay me?" Stepmother hissed.

"You are excused." Father said to the physician. "Now, now, love. Let's not be angry with Mara yet. She may have given me the opportunity I've been searching for since that Calos bitch became queen." He paced the room, scratching his chin. "How does a woman lie with a dragon?" Mara didn't know if it was directed at her, but she had no intention of answering. Gannon's secret was safe with her. "Why did it let you go?"

This one she responded to. "I escaped."

"*The Blackwood Beast* is as cruel a creature as they say then? You appear unharmed to me."

"I encountered no beast."

Stepmother took the birch cane from the wall and tapped it threateningly on her stomach. "What have I told you about lying?"

Father touched her forearm, stalling her. "Do you remember the story of the dragon brides, daughter?"

"No."

"My nursemaid used to tell stories of the stolen maidens. Some would return to their families, as you did, only to be snatched away again. Those that weren't were often excommunicated. Do you know why?"

He paused by the window, pulling back the black curtain to reveal a setting sun. Had it already been so long since she was in bed with Gannon curled around her?

"Their virtue was gone. Dragons have an appetite that matches men. Even with no examination, it was always known by the distinct mark that appeared on their skin. It's been confirmed with my own eyes." He placed a palm on the windowsill, leaning against it. "Queen Sophia bears a similar mark on her neck—dragon's whore. It's no wonder that beast comes at her call. Does king Burne know the child growing inside her is an abomination that belongs not to a man, but a monster?"

With no argument to prove him wrong, Mara uttered the first thing she could think of. "I was willing."

"Of course, you were. Your mother was a useless whore and despite Lucilla's best efforts, you are fruit from the same tree." He sneered. "You will finally serve a purpose in this family. Tell me where the Beast of the Blackwood nests. Or better yet, call him to you the way that bitch calls the gold one. I have sought to capture *the Beast* for nearly ten years and for nearly ten years he has evaded my hunters. It seems I've finally found the perfect bait."

"I don't know how to call him." It was the truth. "I have returned because the beast has lost interest in me."

"Nonsense. They always return for the same woman." Stepmother said.

"A dragon is the type of weapon that guarantees victories, Mara. I need that beast."

She shook her head, refusing her father's request, though she knew what the outcome of her stubbornness would be. "Very well. I'm sure Lucilla can convince you."

The door shut behind Father with a heavy finality, leaving her to face a beaming stepmother. "I do so love our time together, stepdaughter. Nothing eases the stresses of courtly life as much as you." She flexed her fingers on the cane. "I want that dragon, you whore, and you will give it to me."

CHAPTER 18

GANNON

SOMETHING WAS WRONG. GANNON bolted upright, heat flaring in his lungs as smoke coiled from his nostrils. His dragon had woken him, the beast anxiously pacing and insisting that *something was wrong*.

His first instinct was to reach across the bed for Mara. The sheets were cold beside him. She must have shifted away. No, there were only pillows and a messy pile of blankets on the bed.

Well, the hour was late for waking. Perhaps she'd risen to clean herself up or tend to her morning needs. Maybe she was hungry. All the activity from the night before had certainly left him famished. That had to be it. Gannon would come down the stairs to find her breaking her fast, entertained by one or more of his brothers, no doubt.

Wrong. His dragon roared. Some niggling sensation told him that wasn't right.

Focusing inward, Gannon reached out to the newly formed bond between them. It was fragile and fresh, but the emotions shared between them came through just fine. Mara was upset—*anguished*.

And she wasn't here. He couldn't say how he knew but he was sure he wouldn't find her in this house.

His own anguish ripped from him in a roar. Rage quickly followed and he spent it by attacking the space around him. Feathers fluffed through the air and scraps of fabric flew as the bed was his first victim.

Next came a reading chair, a decorative vase, a stack of books that had been sitting on the table since his father was alive. By the time Gannon was done, the room was unrecognizable. The sole part that was wholly intact was the painting above the bed. Green eyes glared out at him, and he cursed them.

How could he be so senseless? Women were not to be trusted. Madeline proved that. Yet Mara wormed her way into his heart so easily. Clearly, he hadn't steeled it well enough.

"Are you done?" Elsie stood with her arms crossed, leaning one shoulder on the jamb of the door.

Snarling, he whirled on her, smoke still churning from his mouth and nose. "You brought her into my home! You brought another lying, manipulating vile—"

She held up a hand. "You will regret that sentence if you finish it. Do you even know where she's gone? Why? With whom?"

"I don't care!" He shouted, closing in on Elsie until they were nose to nose. "She's gone! What does the rest matter?"

Elsie's mouth was open to answer but she never got a word out. A blur of muscle and violence tackled him, fists pounding into him too fast for him to retaliate. The bright orange eyes of a dragon burned down at him, their intent clear. Eoin would kill him if he didn't come to his senses.

In a voice that was very much not his brothers, Eoin growled, "You *dare* to touch her? To speak to her without respect?"

"He didn't touch me, Eoin." Elsie approached, careful to keep her distance.

Gannon finally managed to get in a shot, knocking his brother's head back with a punch to the chin. "Get off me you ugly bastard."

Eoin continued and so did Gannon, grappling for the upper hand, sending elbows and knuckles in every direction. Gannon was strong, but Eoin had the advantage of training and size on his side. Both were panting when his brother slipped behind him, tucking his thick arm around Gannon's throat and cutting off his air. The room began to blur as Gannon scrambled for a breath that wouldn't come.

Ever imprudent, Elsie stomped over and slapped Eoin across the face—hard. "Enough! Both of you!"

Eoin pulled back his lips to reveal lethally pointed teeth. His eyes were a blazing sunset as he growled viciously at Elsie. The moment he registered that it was her who struck him, he stopped. Those eyes lit for a different reason, the growl dying in his throat. With catlike grace he dropped his arm and rose from the floor, prowling toward Elsie.

If Gannon believed her to be truly in danger, he would have intervened. But he recognized the look on his brother's face—it was the same he'd worn the night he discovered Mara in the Blackwood—and it would be a death sentence to come between Eoin and what he clearly saw as his.

"Eoin, it's me."

"He knows." Gannon croaked.

"I know." Eoin purred at the same time. Elsie trembled as he lifted a finger to trace the scar that cut through the middle of her cheek. "Hello, Elsie."

She collected herself quickly, straightening her shoulders and chiding, "I don't want to clean blood from that rug. If you plan to kill your brother, you best do it outside."

"Don't look at him." He hissed.

Confused, Elsie did exactly that, glancing over Eoin's shoulder to frown at Gannon. Eoin caught her chin, tilting it up with a harsh, "If you look at him again there will be blood."

Elsie smacked his hand away. "I have had enough of you Black brothers and your atrocious manners. Both of you get your heads on straight and start worrying about Mara."

"She left!" Gannon meant for it to sound incensed, but it came out as a pathetic groan. "She bound herself to me then left."

"And you haven't got a clue why?" Elsie prodded. Suddenly she was shrieking as Eoin gripped her by the hips and lifted her off the ground, carrying her from the room. "What has gotten into you? Put me down you scoundrel!" It was clear by the scuffling sounds that came from the hall that she was fighting him. By the satisfied rumble that filled the air, Eoin liked it.

Gannon couldn't say he was surprised that Elsie was Eoin's mate. Quite the contrary. For years he'd thought surely fate got it wrong by not pairing the two of them together. Now he was more perplexed than ever. It was no wonder Eoin was like an animal caged in his own skin. He found his mate *ten years* ago and never claimed her. That was an explanation Gannon would be demanding from his brother very soon.

As soon as he was done doing whatever it was he was doing to Elsie.

With a cry, Gannon leapt up from the floor, clutching his chest as his heart snapped with the sudden rush of pain that came through the bond. There was a thump and seconds later Elsie reappeared, a pale and sweating Eoin trailing behind her. The color of his eyes had returned to its normal shade, but the set of his jaw told Gannon he wasn't finished warring with his dragon. Gannon made a point to avoid looking directly at Elsie, instead focusing on his brother.

"She's in pain." Who was hurting her? They would *burn*.

"I imagine that royal father of hers wasn't pleased with her for becoming a wayward bride."

"Why would she be with her father?"

"If you two ruffians would behave rationally for a heartbeat, I will explain it to you." Quieter, she muttered, "Men are all idiots." Eoin cleared his throat, provoking an angry finger from Elsie. "You don't say a word. Scoundrel."

"Explain?" Gannon said a touch too loud, making Eoin's upper lip twitch with a stifled snarl. "You knew she meant to go home?"

"I found out this morning, same as you. It was Edgar who saw her off."

"I'm going to strangle that little weasel—"

"You'll do no such thing!" Eoin stepped closer when Elsie raised her voice. "Think hard about exactly what message you received from the king yesterday, Gannon."

"What's that got to do with Mara leaving?"

"If you discovered your presence risked the execution of the one you loved, how would you respond? If a war was to be wrongfully fought in your name?"

The blood drained from Gannon's face. He would do exactly as Mara did, even if it meant facing the consequences she was clearly facing from her family. Another jolt of pain—she was trying to muffle it from him, he could tell—snapped him back to the present.

"I'm going to retrieve her."

"How?" Eoin spoke up gruffly. "You can't just fly in there and attack the castle."

"I can. I will." He found his shirt on the floor and pulled it over his head.

"If they see you take her, what's to stop them from coming after you? What's to stop her from fleeing again in fear for your safety?" Eoin asked. "You'll need to be strategic. There needs to be no reason for the king or anyone else to pursue her. They must believe she is irretrievable."

Elsie scowled. "You bring that girl back in one piece or you will hear it from me."

"She'll be fine." His brother assured. "But it's going to be difficult to find her, much less snatch her after they believe her taken once already."

"Difficult is fine. Whatever it takes." Mara was in pain because of him. *For* him. She loved him so she was willing to return to the prison she was raised in. That was the kind of heart she had. How could he ever have doubted her?

"I'm going to put on a fresh pot of tea. I think we'll need it." Elsie turned to leave.

"We?" Eoin's brows lifted slightly. "You won't be involved in this campaign."

"You should know by now not to argue with me, Eoin Black," was her parting remark.

"She's right. No use arguing." Gannon sighed, readjusting his pants and preparing to follow her to the east wing. As he passed Eoin, he murmured, "*That* is why you've been an insufferable prick. You can't ignore your mate forever."

Eoin looked as if he wanted to deny it but couldn't physically bring himself to utter the words. "Worry about *your* mate."

With his back to his brother, Gannon said, "She pines for you when you're gone, you know. Every day she stares at that gate as if you'll come riding home."

Eoin shoved him on his way by. "If I'm going to risk my neck for your mate, I expect you to keep yours out of my business."

Gannon watched his brother storm down the hall, wide shoulders nearly knocking the paintings and sconces as he went. Very well. He couldn't control Eoin or dictate his life. The only subject he needed occupying his mind right now was Mara. He was prepared to do anything to bring her home.

CHAPTER 19

AFTER HOURS OF ARGUING that ended with Gannon tossing the dining room table in frustration, there was still no plan. His brothers were well versed in strategy, but they were not preparing for battle. Surely it couldn't be this complicated to walk into the castle, locate Mara, and steal her away. From there it would be simple. He could follow his original plan: forge her an identity as a foreigner and take her as his wife.

"And how do you expect to gain entry to the castle?" Amos had inquired, his tone much less demanding than Eoin's.

"I'm a baron! My attendance at court is not out of the ordinary."

"After a decade absence, it is very much out of the ordinary." Davin pointed out.

"I've had enough of this." He went to kick one of the toppled plates and thought better of it. It was bad enough that he'd wrecked the Baron chamber. Destroying his whole house would do nothing to quell his burning fury. "I'm going to bring my mate home."

His brothers followed as he marched out the front doors and began stripping from his clothes.

"You're an idiot." Davin snorted.

"At least take a horse." Amos begged.

Eoin finished their henpecking with, "You can't go walking through the capital of Dunhill naked."

A fair point. They made plenty, however, and he simply couldn't adhere to their rules. Mara was no longer in pain, but what he felt from her was worse. There was a coldness seeping from her into the bond, as if all the beauty that defined her was being locked away. She was out of reach not only in person but in their bond. He couldn't take it any longer.

"You can follow on the road. Bring a horse for me." He made a final statement before letting the dragon take his skin.

The beast was determined, his every instinct honed on Mara. In this form it was easy to track her, the feeling of her an ever-growing pulse in the distance. The Blackwood was a sea of grey and green below him. His journey was short, shorter than he remembered the distance between his estate and castle Dunhill. The swift beat of his wings carried him past the gates and up around the towers.

Ten years away from the capital and it took him only ten minutes to return by flight. *Ten minutes* was the amount of time it would have taken him to reach the mate that was separated from him only by a forest and a wall of stone. In his neglect of his duties, he'd prevented himself from finding her sooner. What if he could have protected her from the worst of the torment? Stolen her away before all of this nonsense? He would never, *never* let himself retreat so deeply again.

Shouts and shrieks were carried to him on the wind. He paid them no mind. Mara was near. Now it was just a matter of reaching her. Perhaps, he thought, his brothers were right. The longer he circled the castle, the more furious he became. There was nowhere for him to land where he might shift and make his way into the castle and there was no way for this form to make an entrance. She was within his grasp, and he couldn't reach her.

His roar drowned out the shrill cries of women and the crying of startled children. The noise echoed across the open sky.

Gannon was about to turn back toward the Blackwood and locate his brothers when the unthinkable happened. Guards poured from the main castle doors to fill the courtyard. They preceded a small flock of well-dressed men. Obvious among them was the king, his crown a gold wreath around his head. Following closely behind him were two women. One was dressed in a gown of blue—the queen. The other wore a vibrant red, catching the eye amid the beige and silver of soldier's garb.

Mara. There she was, presented to him like a beautifully wrapped gift.

Unlike the queen, she did not carry herself with poise and grace. Mara had soldiers at her back, forcing her forward as she thrashed and kicked.

The logical part of his mind recognized that something was amiss. But it was not that part of him that ruled currently. His mate was here, wounded and captive, and he intended to retrieve her. With an exuberant roar he dove downward, landing in the courtyard with a thunderous boom. Soldiers shifted and wavered in place. The king's guard was made of fiercer stuff, closing ranks around the royal family as Gannon stretched his wings in a threatening display.

Mara met his gaze. Her face was pale, her eyes sunken. She'd been transformed back into the lifeless puppet who sat politely in his study while he growled at her. It was so wrong it made him ill to see.

Instead of the joy and relief he hoped to see, Mara flailed wildly and snarled, "you should not have come! Leave, beast!"

The queen began shaking her by the arm, trying to silence Mara as she screamed to him. Her urgency only stirred him more. But as he prepared to advance on the soldiers, pain exploded in his right wing. Gannon whipped around to face the foe and found a large metal bolt puncturing the leathery skin. It had sharp arms that protruded from its center, clinging to his wing. Six soldiers rushed to secure the bottom of it to a massive hook. He tried to turn teeth on them, but it was already fastened, linking the weapon to a thick chain even he would struggle against. Any sudden movements and the bolt would shred his wing, leaving irreparable damage.

In his distraction he didn't see the second bolt as he was thrust into his other wing, pinning him in place. He thrashed his head back and forth, snapping at those in reach, but it was no use. The soldiers swarmed him like ants, fastening chains all about his body. Gannon released a burst of fire from his throat, but it was cut short as a heavy net made of chain was shoved over his snout. He was not even given the dignity to roar in outrage.

Mara was covering her mouth, tears glittering on her rosy cheeks. She was horrified and fearful, but the one emotion he couldn't get past was her guilt. Why did she feel so guilty?

Had she...had she done this to him? Aided her father? Was this all a trick to capture the Beast of the Blackwood and add him to her father's menagerie?

That suspicion seemed to be confirmed as the king approached Gannon with a delighted laugh, his eyes sparkling like a boy on Christmas morning. "Very well done, daughter. Very well done indeed. *This* is the kind of weapon I've been waiting for." The king stretched a cautious hand out to touch Gannon's head. Gannon could do nothing but growl. There were chains around his neck, chains securing his feet—more metal than he'd ever seen in one place. "You'll learn to serve me, beast. My sweet Mara will make sure of it."

Gannon's eyes found those irises of soft brown. He thought he saw so much in them—thought he saw his future! But now he couldn't see her clearly, couldn't judge truth from fictitious stories told to gain his sympathy. He'd heard them before, been wrapped so tightly around another woman's finger that he couldn't breathe. Had Mara used that? Was she so cruel and heartless?

She didn't look it on the outside, didn't act like it when she was in his home. But here she stood, watching as he was shackled like a prisoner. Gannon closed his eyes, unable to bear the pain any longer. It wasn't the throb in his wings nor the weight of the chains, it was the feel of his heart shattering into a thousand unsalvageable pieces.

<hr>

Betrayed.

That was how Gannon looked. That was how he felt across their bond. Mara knew little else but his betrayal. Even the pain as his wings dripped steaming blood onto the courtyard was muted beneath that one poisonous feeling.

How could he believe she would willingly do this? Mara was ready to sacrifice herself for his life and he believed her capable of this horror? She couldn't bear to look upon him any longer. Not as he bled and groaned under the weight of imprisonment. So desperate was she to keep him safe that she'd been imprudent in her planning. Of course, he would come after her, and look at the results.

Mara was unable to free herself. How would she ever free Gannon?

Gods, it hurt to see what they'd done to him as much as it hurt to see him turn away from her. Those beautiful black wings were stretched too far apart. Could they recover from such an injury? Surely it wouldn't do permanent damage if father intended to use the dragon as a weapon of war. She shuddered at the thought. By what means did her father plan to break Gannon?

Mara had come here expecting exactly what she received: punishment and a promise that her marriage to a man of her father's choosing was imminent. But she hadn't anticipated Gannon being here. Perhaps she knew that he would feel betrayed by her and secretly hoped that would keep him away. She wanted one night with him, a single night to be selfish, and then she would leave him to believe what he would about her, so long as it meant he lived.

To be imprisoned was not living, however. To be tortured and molded into a means for violence was not living. And sooner or later Gannon would die. If not at the hands of her father, it would be by the fangs of the Calos dragon. Gannon was fierce, but there wasn't enough ferocity in the world to match the two dragons in size and strength. Gannon was built for swiftness, to be a sly and silent hunter. The dragon of Calos was a berserker in comparison.

A powerful purpose rose up like flames inside of her, burning away the frosty numbness. Whether or not he wanted her after what she'd done, Mara would set Gannon free. She wouldn't allow her father to cage and use him the way he had her.

CHAPTER 20

MARA

THERE WAS TO BE a party in celebration of the new addition to father's menagerie. A party to celebrate a war that was to be declared come springtime, a war the court believed would be won because of their new weapon. *The Beast of the Blackwood.*

Weeks had gone by, and Mara saw nothing of Gannon. She felt him, though. No matter how much love and comfort she tried to send to him, how much she thought longingly of him, their bond was polluted with rage. She couldn't really blame him. Wherever he was in the depths of the castle, it was no better than her new living quarters.

Stepmother had servants move a cot into the tower room where Mara received her punishments. Lucilla had only been by three times in so many weeks, but the room was punishment enough. Mara took her meals there, slept there, and spent her days there. She was given no clothing but a thin nightdress and no blanket to cover herself with during the long, cold nights. Those were the times she craved the heat of Gannon's body beside her most.

At one point she considered taking the curtain down from the narrow window and using it to cover herself, but stepmother would likely confiscate it if she found out. The curtain provided a finite amount of defense against the biting wind, at least.

This morning was the first she'd left that dreadful stone room since Gannon was captured. It was a struggle not to rush to the blaze in the fireplace and put her hands as close as they could get without burning them. The determination that kept her warm for so many nights was waning as she feared she would never be allowed to leave the tower again. Now it was rekindled, fire eating up newfound hope like dry wood. Even as she felt Gannon grow less furious and more defeated, she held fast. She would set him free yet.

Stepmother spent nearly an hour griping at handmaids. She hissed in Mara's direction too, an angry snake ready to strike if Mara so much as breathed improperly. There was far too much gossip and speculation about her absence at court, thus she was required to attend the *dragon feast*, as it was being called.

There were so many rules it made her head spin. Though Mara had been at the Black estate for only two short months, she'd quickly unlearned all the intricacies of court socializing. Elsie was right. It was all nonsense and she felt completely fettered by it.

The gown selected for her evening attire was more conservative than usual. Scars from her punishment were carefully left below the collar so that none would show while she was in regular attire. Gannon's mark, however, was not so easily disguised. Stepmother picked a dress in the current winter style. The waist of the dress was raised to below her bust, giving the appearance of longer and more slender legs. Female figures were expected to be lean and lithe. Plush hips had lost their fashion appeal and now all the ladies at court wore gowns meant to make them seem lighter than they were.

Modesty was an important virtue, but none were dressed as modestly as Mara. The neck of her dress came halfway up her throat. She felt collared by it and wanted to rip open the buttons and take a gasping breath.

Women and men alike murmured as she walked into the great hall. Their first comments were on her dress—a sleek onyx that reminded her of Gannon's wings as they shimmered in the sunlight. Black was a color of mourning, and it was meant to show that she was still recovering from her "ordeal," but Mara wondered if there was a subtle hint at her connection to the dragon, too.

She hadn't been privy to the rumors that were floating around about her. Tonight, she became familiar with all of them. There were some who believed the king's story completely and thought Mara a helpless victim. Others whispered about a lover that abandoned Mara after she agreed to run away with him. Unsurprisingly, the worst of the rumors were uttered by men.

Women were often labeled as petty gossips, yet the women in her father's court were taught never to speak ill of others or to even think of impure topics like the one being discussed loudly behind her. At least not in mixed company.

"Kidnapped? That's not what I heard." A drunken lord of something or other boasted. "I heard she went willing with Calos soldiers. Heard she lay with each of them before they discarded her back here. No one wants a used up woman."

"If I'd known it was so easy to get a princess to spread her legs, I'd have stolen one ages ago!" Their laughter was raucous and grating. She was so fixated on tuning them out that she didn't hear the person speaking beside her.

"Are you well, princess?" Gods, it was Lord Wyman.

"I am. Thank you. And you, my lord?"

"I have been better." He sipped from his goblet of wine. "Is it true, what they've said about your disappearance?"

"That depends greatly on which 'they' you are referring to." She answered shortly.

"Forgive me, I meant no offense." By all appearances, Lord Wyman was a peaceful man. He would have made a decent husband. But Mara could never have loved someone that was not her choice. Now she would never love again. Her heart would always belong to Gannon, no matter if he abandoned her the way he believed her to have abandoned him. "I was eager to be wed to you, though we'd only just met."

Mara didn't know what to say, so she simply nodded. "I am not a particularly pious man, nor am I restrained by the biases of the court, generally speaking. I could never begrudge a woman the loss of her maidenhead outside of marriage were it not her choice."

"I beg your pardon?"

"What I'm trying to say, princess, is that I would still have you as my wife, so long as you agree to be faithful and obedient. My family is very wealthy, and your father will need our support for his coming war."

Faithful and obedient. *Obedient.* Why was that the expectation of a wife? When women like Queen Sophia and Elsie were out there? They had tongues as bold as men and bravery that, in Mara's opinion, surpassed a man's. No one would tell Queen Sophia to be obedient. Even Eoin wouldn't dare ask obedience of Elsie.

The mask that she wore so carefully during her life at court had broken while she was with Gannon. Though her stepmother had fastened it back on, the cracks still showed. The facade was not thick enough to cover up the woman she'd become—the woman she'd always been when she wasn't confined to a cage.

"You wish me to obey you?"

Lord Wyman was caught off guard by her question. "As any good wife should."

"A dog obeys." She challenged. "Does a woman not deserve autonomy? Or do you want a doll rather than a wife?"

The boisterous gossipers behind them had gone unusually quiet. Obviously, eavesdropping was another of their pastimes. The exchange was devolving quickly when they were interrupted by a looming shadow and a gruff, commanding voice she'd already come to know well.

"Princess, forgive the interruption. Your father requires your presence."

"A man of house Black with manners." Mara said for his benefit. "How unexpected."

Eoin huffed, taking her arm less gently than a true gentleman would and leading her away.

"Eoin? What are you doing here?" Mara whispered, following him without a second glance.

Eoin was always stiff and stern, but the response that came from him now was downright frigid. "My brother is abed with a fever and required me to attend in his stead."

"What of Davin and Amos? Are they here too?" She knew her questions weren't well received but she continued anyway. "Tell me of Elsie. How is she faring? Edgar and Nigel too."

"You almost sound as if you care." Too late Mara realized Eoin was leading her not toward the head table where father was seated beside his two favorite lords, but to a doorway used mainly by servants. She glanced back to see if anyone was watching their exit, but Eoin was careful to take her in a wide circle of the room, avoiding Lord Wyman and other prying eyes.

"Of course, I care."

"Then why is my brother in chains?" He growled, yanking her through the doorway and pushing her roughly against the wall. His pupils became fine black lines, and his eyes glowed the color of a sunset in the dim hall.

Amos and Davin were silent as they flanked her. Both sported the eyes of their dragons too. Davin's were a shade of blue that would be breathtaking were they not glaring menacingly down at her. Surprisingly, it was Amos that was most the threatening of the three. His irises bled a violent red, his face was transformed into a snarl.

"What have you done?" Amos demanded gruffly.

"I have done nothing and that is my greatest failure." Her words shook with her fear, but she held her head high. "I never intended for him to follow me here."

"I was there when they took him." Eoin hissed. "I heard your father congratulating you on your success."

"Because he knows what I am! He saw Gannon's mark and knew what it meant. I would *never* see him caged."

Davin breathed out loudly between his lips, startling her with the noise. His eyes returned to their usual black and his lips were kicked up into a half smile. "I believe her."

"I don't care if you believe me or not." Mara tossed her arms up, feeling suddenly furious. Gannon's impotent rage had been eating at her day and night. Paired with her guilt it was becoming a whirling storm inside of her. "I was ready to forfeit my own life and happiness to keep him safe! Think what you will of me, but I am going to set him free, and my only chance is tonight. Do not make me lose this opportunity."

"And how exactly do you plan to do that?" Eoin was no longer vibrating with hostility, but his tone hadn't changed and his eyes vacillating between black and sunset orange, his pupils thinning and stretching.

She blew out a sigh. "I haven't figured that out yet. My father plans to reveal him in the courtyard when the feast is finished. I thought perhaps I could sneak away during the feast and unchain him."

"Impossible. He's not currently in the courtyard and we haven't been able to locate where they're keeping him. Besides, those chains likely weigh more than three grown men if they're keeping Gannon in check. You would never be able to lift them." Amos rubbed his jaw thoughtfully. "We'll need a distraction."

It wasn't the first time Mara had heard that suggestion hours before a celebratory feast. The words sparked an idea, and she clapped her hands together excitedly. "We'll need dragons."

"What?"

"*More* dragons." She explained to them how she escaped during the feast meant to celebrate her upcoming nuptials. The dragon had been docile then, a great beast putting on a show for his doting queen. Tonight, they needed a much more threatening presence.

"No. Out of the question." Eoin was vehement.

"It's a brilliant plan, Eoin, and better than any we've come up with." Davin argued.

"Neither Amos nor I can do it." They locked eyes, an unspoken exchange passing between them. "You know why."

"That's fine." Mara cut in. "As you said, I would need help with the chains anyway. We require only one dragon to cause a stir." She adjusted the suffocating collar of her dress impatiently. "I have to return to the party. My father will notice my absence. If I am under his scrutiny, this will never work."

Eoin was clearly unhappy with the plan, but Amos and Davin were in full support. "Eoin and I will meet you in the courtyard after the feast. We'll need to move quickly, so be ready."

"Of course." She nodded, hurrying to the door. Just before opening it, Mara turned and warned, "My father has a weapon. You must avoid it Davin. I don't know quite how it works, but it will take out your wings." She swallowed bile. "I pray Gannon will still be able to fly, else our plan may be useless."

Mara was so distracted with worry over the events to come that she didn't think to check before exiting the servant's hall. She made it only three steps before colliding with Lord Wyman.

"There you are! What are you doing in there? Planning to flee another party?" His amicable expression was gone, jaw set harshly. He wasn't a large man, but he was certainly imposing when he had her cornered.

Was there any use keeping up her father's lies? Perhaps it was wise to continue for now. "I was only hoping to sneak a peek at the dragon, but it seems my father is hiding him away."

"I suppose I should consider myself fortunate that our wedding was disrupted." He sneered. "A woman that lies so easily must have filthy secrets to hide."

On cue all three Black brothers appeared through the doorway, not expecting her to still be lingering nearby. Lord Wyman looked them up and down, his sneer growing as his took in Amos' and Davin's soldier uniforms.

"The rumors are true, aren't they? Your father will be lucky to marry you to a boar." He accented his parting words by spitting on the front of her dress.

Mara stared after him, her jaw hanging loose. How quickly the courtiers turned against her based on rumors and lies. What point was there to all the etiquette and niceties when it was false? A veneer to make a pit of vipers look like an inviting garden. She'd had enough of it. The poison was rotting in her guts, sickening her. No matter what happened tonight, no matter if Gannon shunned her for the rest of her days, she would not stay here—*could not.*

Whether she escaped and became a beggar girl in some faraway city or threw herself from the window in her tower, she was *finished.*

"Don't worry." Davin handed her a handkerchief as he passed. "I'll make sure to eat him first."

CHAPTER 21

MARA

I T TOOK EVERY WELL practiced ounce of self-control to keep from fidgeting during dinner. Mara's legs were filled with skittering bugs, and she desperately wanted to bounce them. But stepmother was seated to her right, an important lord and his wife to her left, and she knew better than to draw their attention. Act the part, be the poor, tarnished princess for one more night. Then one way or another, it would end.

That ending couldn't come soon enough.

Her gaze was fixed on her plate for most of dinner, mindlessly chewing and sipping wine only to keep up appearances. The food had no taste, and the texture may as well have been rubber for all that it registered to her. Only once did she risk a glance to the far table to see Eoin seated with a collection of other wealthy barons. That seat had been empty during every feast and celebration for as long as Mara could remember. If Gannon's father once occupied that table, sharing in conversation and laughing genially, she couldn't remember.

Those were the beginning days of her training, though, and much of it was a blur. Mara hadn't yet come to terms with the behavior of her new mother nor the fact that her father allowed it. She was too young to learn how to numb herself to the mistreatment.

Now that she had Gannon's fire in her veins, she may never be able to numb herself again. Her body burned too hot; her soul lined with the magic that made him what he was. Even so far away from him, kept apart by distance and miscommunication, she could feel how he blazed with life. A bonfire embodied within a man—sometimes too hot, too fierce, but comforting when she was cold and weary.

Gods what she would give to warm herself with his fire again, if only one last time.

Father stood when he'd finished gorging himself on the three extravagant courses. He gave a long-winded speech about power and strength. On and on he went, mentioning enemies he dreamed up while pretending to handle disputes between landowners and requests for subsidies from struggling farmers. The only time the King of Dunhill sounded eloquent was when he spoke of war. Father waxed poetic about battle and destruction, painting an image of carnage and rallying the court for an impending fight that none of them would be participating in.

It was merely a game to them. A round of chess with living, breathing pieces and far more intriguing stakes than the pride of winning or the shame of losing.

"I know your fears, good sirs." He straightened his gold filigree doublet. "To that I say, fear not. Your king has a weapon that will win us this war and all the wars to come." Murmurs rippled through the hall and father grinned. "Indeed, the rumors are true. Let me show you my prize."

Father led the march to the courtyard, lords, barons, and wealthy merchants in tow. The women followed politely behind, their posture perfect and their hands clasped. Mara could see the electric excitement spreading through him as they fought not to fidget and whisper to one another. Stepmother walked primly beside Mara, her eyes narrowed suspiciously. Avoiding her attention was of the utmost importance if their plan was to work.

She feigned meekness, slumping her shoulders and casting her eyes down. The show worked. By the time they reached the courtyard, Lucilla was hurrying to join Father, beaming with twisted excitement.

The courtyard was lit with hundreds of torches, the crackling of the flames lending a foreboding energy to the atmosphere. Shadows cast across faces by the flickering lights did the same, masking half of her father's expression and giving him an eerie smile. The stage was set for a grand reveal. He would be furious if it didn't go as he expected.

Mara intended to make sure it wouldn't.

The rattling of chains was the first noise that caught the attention of the courtiers. Collective breath was held as a gargantuan shadow began to take shape. It lumbered to the center of the courtyard, led by a team of leather clad animal handlers, as if a dragon was no different than the tigers and bears father kept in the menagerie. How could they miss the intelligence in those stunning emerald eyes?

Eyes that looked empty and defeated until they locked on her. It wasn't love shining in those beautiful twin emeralds. It was hatred.

Mara convinced herself that she could live with Gannon hating her for leaving. She couldn't. Her heart ceased to beat as he watched her with nothing but predatory malice. The chains around his neck and legs added to the burden of her ache. His shame and humiliation was immense and she wanted nothing more than to take it from him.

The metal netting around his mouth kept it firmly closed, guaranteeing there would be no guests cooked up and served as a fourth course. Father stepped brazenly close to Gannon and waved his arms theatrically. "I present to you, the Beast of the Blackwood."

There were gasps and whispers of horror and awe. Wives turned to their husbands to cower in their arms. One woman grew woozy and lost her footing. To them, they were looking upon a novelty. A monstrosity. Mara saw only the man that held her as she lost her wits in the maze. The man who shared his most precious places with her. The man whose flesh had come into her and claimed her.

"I love you." She whispered. Gannon's hearing was better than an ordinary man's, but she hadn't expected him to hear her over the crowd as they raged with questions. His head whipped in her direction though, obvious enough that father shot her a brief but scathing glare.

"How will you control it?"

"I have excellent means of persuasion." Another glance from him in her direction and Mara shuddered. "And I've already been teaching the creature that I am his master. He eats only twice per week, and it is my hand that delivers his meal. I've seen it work a hundred times to tame the untamable. A dragon is, after all, simply an animal."

Idiot. He would never train a dragon the way he did a tiger. Gannon was so much more.

Mara inched closer and closer to the front of the courtyard as the king boasted to the courtiers about his prowess and dominance over predators of the fiercest nature. More than once he risked a quick touch to Gannon's neck, only to retreat when he heard a rumble of warning or felt the heat of his scales. An angry dragon was a hot dragon, as evidenced by the smoke coming from Gannon's nostrils.

She was mere feet away from him now, aching to touch him. The bolts had been removed from his wings. There was obvious scarring where they entered but it didn't look as though it would hurt his ability to fly. Father wouldn't have utilized such a weapon if it would immobilize his *prize*.

"These," Father gestured to those very bolts, sitting on display beneath a ring of torches. "Are a gift from the Gazari king. I've recently entered a unique agreement with him and to thank me, he has aided us in acquiring a dragon of our own. The royal family of Gazar has kept a dragon for more than a hundred years. Imagine that! One day

I may pass this dragon down onto my sons." A bold statement since stepmother had yet to birth a son that lived. He stepped away from the dragon and touched the top of one bolt. "They are designed to take a dragon down without causing a lethal wound. With the right equipment, soldiers could launch them into the sky and drop an enemy dragon." Like Burne in Calos. Mara made a mental note to send a letter of warning to Queen Sophia should she ever gain the freedom to do so.

Eoin quietly slipped in behind her. His breath moved her hair as he muttered, "It's almost time."

Gannon, who had never taken his eyes off of her, shifted his shoulders in agitation. The presence of his brother perplexed him.

"I'm ready." She answered through clenched teeth.

So was Davin as he swooped above them. If not for the stream of fire that arched from his lips, he would have been invisible in the night sky—a dragon shaped hole cut out from the stars. Most were too fixated on her father's showboating to immediately notice the anomalous fire.

Mara helped them along by pointing upward and screaming as loud as she could. "Dragon! There's another dragon!"

The king and queen were the only ones to look to her and not the sky, suspicion evident. They too lost their focus on her as Davin dove low over the courtyard, trumpeting angrily.

"Now." Eoin nudged her. He and Amos were already hurrying over to the anchors that held the chains in place.

Davin blew out another burst of fire, this time close enough to singe the grass in the courtyard. Courtiers scattered in all directions, some making for the castle and others running beyond the torches, hoping to use darkness as cover. Mara ran in the opposite direction, her sight set on the net covering Gannon's snout.

A sudden sharp tug on the back of her head snapped her neck backward. "Don't you dare! You will not take this from us." Stepmother had her hand tangled in Mara's hair. The other came up to slap her face hard enough to make her vision stutter.

But it was Lucilla who had taken so much from Mara. Her innocence. Her joy and her peace. Mara spent years living as nothing more than a pretty prop to be staged at social events and traded into marriage. She wouldn't let Stepmother take Gannon from her too.

Mara slammed her elbow backward, meeting ribs and causing a groan. The heel of her boot stomped down on Lucilla's foot. She swiftly raised it again, kicking the shin behind hers and finally causing Stepmother to lose her grip. As soon as she was free, Mara spun. She slapped Lucilla once, twice, thrice. The third hit knocked her backwards. Mara took advantage of her stumble, kicking her hard in the ribs where her elbow had previously hit. It was violent and unladylike, and she loved every second of it.

Mara left her tormentor on the ground and ran at Gannon. Amos had two chains undone and was going for the oversized bolt on a third, giving Gannon more freedom to move his neck. She had to dodge as he swung it toward her, nearly smashing her as he writhed.

"Not yet!" Eoin shouted. "Hold still."

"Soldiers! Stop them!" Father barked from where he stood over the queen. "And seize the princess!"

Gannon dipped his head as Mara reached him. Her fingers fiddled with the chain netting, trying to find the mechanism that fastened it. She found a narrow pin and pulled it. The net loosened but didn't drop from his face. She pulled another and another. Just as the netting was falling free a hand grabbed her foot, yanking her backward and onto her belly. She gripped the netting as she fell, sliding it from Gannon's mouth.

Then everything was burning. A wall of flame cut off the remaining soldiers and the escaping courtiers. Gannon expanded his wings and lifted his front legs before slamming them down onto the ground and scorching more of the courtyard with his blazing breath.

Mara could scarcely see through the smoke and blinding firelight. Her gown was aflame, but she was too focused on staying upright to feel the heat. Feet scurried by and bodies were dragged out of Gannon's reach. Peripherally she saw his brothers backing away and realized she was alone on the ground before the dragon. She pressed up onto her arms, staring at the beast that loomed over her. The look in his eyes was unreadable, his emotions equally muddled. Would he end her for her assumed betrayal? Had he already had a taste of that heartache and couldn't stomach more?

A clawed foot landed too close to her legs, grazing the fabric of her dress and gusting the fire out until it was mere sparks. Smoke snaked from the snout that dropped inches from her face. Behind her there was an unnatural stillness as every man and woman stopped to watch in horror as the Beast of the Blackwood descended on the princess. They were too transfixed to notice the second dragon was nowhere to be found.

Searching deeply inside her, she tried to read his emotions. They were scattered, each of them overshadowed by rage. He was so angry to have been chained. Mara understood that anger very well.

Mustering her finite bravery, she looked up at him and reminded him of that night on the balcony. "I promised I wouldn't hurt you." She meant it down to her bones.

Time stilled as the Beast opened his lethal maw and struck at the princess.

CHAPTER 22

MARA

M ARA SHIVERED DESPITE THE heat of scales pressed against her. Winter was at their doorstep and the wind coming off the mountains was viciously cold. Gannon clutched her close to his chest, whether it was to hold her safe or keep her out of sight for any onlooker who might have especially sharp vision, she couldn't say. Even if they saw her, no one would imagine she was alive after what they'd witnessed.

It was likely the only way she could truly be free of her family. Mara didn't know if Gannon planned for her to die by his fangs or if he'd seized the opportunity when it presented itself. To anyone remaining in the courtyard after the dragon attack, it appeared as if the Beast of the Blackwood had broken her. There was a brief moment of fear as his teeth closed around her body. Would Gannon really kill her?

She chose to believe he wouldn't—chose to trust him. With a cry, Mara let her body go limp, impaled on the teeth of a monstrous dragon. Gannon made the show more believable with the growl that shook the ground, his head moving carefully back and forth as if he were finishing the kill. Then he dropped her from his mouth, snatched her up in his hand, and shot into the sky.

The takeoff was shakier than she remembered, and Mara worried it was due to the damage in his wings. She thanked the Gods fiercely that he was airborne.

Gannon was careful when he landed, setting her on her feet before touching down. His caution didn't stop her wobbling legs from collapsing under her.

Here they were again. The garden was haunting and empty in the starlight. Gannon towered over her; those sharp eyes boring into her. Mara was bowed at his feet, completely at his mercy. Her fate was up to him. She didn't speak. There were few words she could give him that would change the outcome of her choices. She'd already said what mattered most.

I love you.

The dragon began shimmering the way the surface of water glittered under the sun. Mara knew what Gannon was, but to see him transform before her eyes was awe inspiring.

"You're beautiful." She murmured.

"I prefer ferocious." Gannon huffed.

"Ferociously beautiful." Truly, he was. Sweat beaded on his muscled chest. His pale skin was painted silver by the half moon.

Neither of them moved. Gannon took deep, unsteady breaths. Mara searched his face, waiting for anger and vitriol—waiting for anything that wasn't this stony silence.

His words finally came in a guttural growl. "You left."

"I had to."

"I would have found a way to keep you safe!"

Mara pushed off from the ground. "It wasn't *my* safety I was concerned with."

"I'm a dragon! I can protect the both of us."

"Can you? Without revealing what you are? If my father discovered I was here, what would you have done? Turned into a dragon and eaten him?" She planted her fists on her hips. "A dragon is not invincible. My father proved that!"

He stepped closer, coming nose to nose with her. "I had a plan, Mara! I had a plan to keep you from him. You shouldn't have left."

"You shouldn't have come after me." She countered.

"I had no choice!"

"Of course, you had a choice."

His hand darted out, catching her under the jaw and forcing her head up. The dragon was returning, his pupils thin strikes of black, irises clouding with green. "You are bound to me. I cannot be complete without you by my side. There wasn't a choice for me. There will never be a choice for me, Mara. I thought you understood that."

Pain. He was in so much pain. Because to him, Mara had abandoned him. Her betrayal was so different than the one he faced before, but it wounded him the same. Truly, she hadn't understood it. She hadn't grasped how thoroughly and indelibly they were connected until she was away from him.

"Every moment without you was misery. I would have endured a thousand punishments before I would ever endure a day without you." She said, drawing his hand from her jaw and taking it in hers. "I was ready to endure both if it meant no harm would come to you. That decision wasn't made from heinous intent, Gannon. It was made from love. I would sacrifice my own happiness for you again if I had to relive it."

"And I would come for you again."

"Then we're at an impasse."

A sheen of emotion wet his eyes and he glanced down. "Indeed."

"Gannon?" Mara cupped his face. His stubble had grown into a beard in their time apart, soft beneath her fingers. "I'm sorry for how I've hurt you. I would take this pain from you if I could."

He threw his arms around her, crushing her to his chest so tightly she could scarcely breathe. "Never again. Do you understand me? You will never leave this estate again."

"Not even to travel? To walk the woods?"

"Careful, woman. I'll amend it to my bed chamber."

She laughed breathlessly. "You plan to keep me prisoner?"

"No." He pulled back, grabbing her by the nape and kissing her. "You will always have your freedom. So long as you understand you're not free to leave without a word."

"If I leave you a note next time then..."

"I am not amused." His smile said otherwise. "Gods woman, you destroy me."

"I would prefer to make you whole."

He growled, lifting her off her feet. "I'll be whole as soon as I'm inside you."

"Let's spend a week in the baron chamber. I won't require bread and beverage if I have you." She painted his neck with kisses.

"Romantic," He smiled sheepishly as he carried her through the garden. "But not possible."

"Why's that?"

"The baron chamber is in need of a few renovations. Some redecorating wouldn't hurt either."

"What did you do?" She gasped.

"I was angry with you!" Gannon set her in the foyer, caging her against the wall with his arms. "I'm still angry with you." But he kissed her anyway, so deeply that she forgot where she was until a throat cleared loudly.

Mara's cheeks flared when she looked up to see Elsie, Edgar, and Nigel standing in the foyer. Davin was behind them, leaning in the doorway to the dining hall with an apple in his hand and a smirk on his face.

"How did you get here so quickly?" Gannon snarled.

His brother shrugged. "I wasn't quick, I just didn't waste the last hour arguing in the garden."

"I'm glad to see neither of you suffered permanent damage during your captivity." Elsie cocked a hip. "Can we get you anything? Some clothing, perhaps?"

Gannon narrowed his eyes at their audience. "You can get out of my way." He scooped Mara into his arms once more, stomping past the onlookers and hurrying up the stairs.

"You'll have to excuse us." Mara popped her head over his shoulder, smiling abashedly.

They barely made it to Mara's chambers before Gannon was plucking at the buttons of her gown. He made it through five before snarling, "Why does it have so many fucking buttons?" and ripping the front open.

His hands were as searing as she remembered on her skin. Mara welcomed it. She wanted him to mark every inch of her with that heat. This was the greatest happiness she would ever know, and she was too aware of how close she'd come to losing it.

"Are you truly still angry with me?" She was as naked as he and suddenly wary. Making love would not mean he forgave her. Surely this wasn't a parting dalliance and nothing more?

"Not *angry*." He sighed, running his hands through already mussed hair. "But hurt."

"Enough that you would find me undesirable?"

He pressed his cock into her belly. "Clearly I desire you."

She couldn't help but rub against him. "Your body desires mine."

"Don't be fooled, Mara." Gannon laid her tenderly onto the bed, climbing over you. "I desire you in every way a man can want a woman." He pushed into her with a satisfied groan. "You have caused a great deal of trouble and I think I love you all the more for it."

"You love me?" She moaned, lifting her hips to invite more of him inside her.

"I love you." He agreed on a thrust. "And now I intend to make love to you until you've permanently forgotten every word but my name."

That night, she did. Over and over, they came together, clinging to each other in ecstasy. In the moments of stillness that followed they remained close, not daring to let one another go. Lady Fate was wise indeed when she made them a match, Mara thought. Nowhere in the world would bring her as much joy as the place between Gannon's arms.

EPILOGUE

THERE WERE MANY VERSIONS of the story of *the Blackwood Beast* and the princess. All agreed that the history of Dunhill would include that fateful night. What they couldn't decide on was exactly what occurred. Some recalled *The Beast* as a blood thirsty monster, ripping the princess to pieces and leaving scraps for her family to bury. Others thought the princess a witch capable of controlling the dragon with her wicked wiles. A scattered few believed her to be the first dragon bride in decades.

Regardless of her fate, the King of Dunhill did not mourn his daughter. If he could speak, he would not ask for her. But he could not speak, and the royal physician was not hopeful that he ever would again. He was fortunate to have any vision at all. Dragon fire spared no one, not even kings.

Baron Black quietly announced a marriage to a foreign woman six weeks after the dragon attack. The court was too busy debating whether they believed their king fit to rule to notice or care. None bothered with the baron at the base of the mountains. The Black estate was cursed and haunted, or so the story went.

With no impending war on the horizon, the soldiers trained in the northern camps were sent home. For the first time in a decade, all four Black brothers were to live under one roof. There was no telling what chaos would ensue.

The newly titled Baroness Black was a mystery to all. If ever there were guests welcomed into the Black estate—there wouldn't be—they would be graced by the beauty of her melodies as she played songs of undying love. Laughter would echo through the wings and boisterous conversation would fill the dining hall as they supped.

Perhaps someone would mention the tale of the princess and *the Beast* that made her end. They would argue and speculate for hours without tiring. The one detail none of them would get right was arguably the most important.

They both lived happily ever after.

THANK YOU FOR READING!

Want more dragon shifters and fated mates? Start the next book in the series now:

Ready for another fast-burn dragon shifter romance? Join my newsletter and download a Dragon Brides novella with new characters and a standalone story.

Thank you for reading Black Heart! Would you help get my books in the hands of more readers by leaving a review?

A quick note about the book 3: You might be surprised if you move on to Book 3 and find it's NOT about Eoin and Elsie. When I originally wrote this series, I never intended to give the Black Brothers their own stories. SO MANY readers wanted to hear about Eoin and Elsie, but that was after book 3 was already published. If you want to skip ahead to the Black Brothers, you can find Eoin's story in Book 4, Midnight Ruin.

ALSO BY

Dragon Brides Series

Blood Feud
Black Heart
Midnight Ruin
Birthright

Beasts of Barbeaux Bayou

Shroud of Exile

Silver Bullet Security

Relentless

About the Author

Moira Kane is a paranormal romance author who prefers to write stories about the dragon that eats Prince Charming. Each of her books has magic and mayhem, but most importantly, a happily ever after.

When she's not writing, Moira can be found nose-deep in a romance novel or searching the woods for her reclusive husband. A Pacific Northwest native turned Midwest transplant, Moira is happily raising three feral children. Some of her other job titles include baker, tree-hugger, dog whisperer, mushroom enthusiast, and weird homeschool mom.

Learn more about Moira on her website: https://moirakane.com/

Instagram: @moirawritesromance

TikTok: @moirawritesromance